# PRETTY

## Her Introduction

Netta B.

# DEDICATION

To my family friend's idols and enemies, all of you motivated me in so many ways and I love you all for it. But the grace of GOD is something I cannot deny, the size of a mustard seed. Enjoy

.

# CONTENTS

To rid the world of pedophiles is a privilege but to rid the world of my offenders is my mission...

Netta B.

.

# Chapter One

Vengeance: infliction of punishment in return for a wrong committed. Yep, that's one way the dictionary puts it. In my opinion vengeance is sweet and bitter, empty or full desire seeking fulfillment. It's a longing type of desire completed with gratification a sweet treat, payback. Setting up the most perfect get back varies in the methods used. See with vengeance you sometimes let the receiving end think they are in the clear out of sight out of mind, but we all know that's a lie especially with feelings involved.

Why does one seek vengeance? Simply put, because a bitch done fucked up! They done fucked with you, your family, money or all. I mean they all kind of intertwine. Messing with either can fuck with your heart and mind, and who likes those two things played with? Why is it always someone who thinks they have the upper hand, as well as the mega master plan? When in theory they just digging up their own fucked up hand. Vengeance, it's my life it's my story. I got a couple of vengeance or had a couple of vengeance. Shit I thought I had a vendetta but I grew to learn it wasn't that deep. Either way I wanna share my story it aint no love story, no sob story, or even inspiring story, it's my story a true story a story I been living and still the fuck is.

Let me introduce myself before I tell any more of my business. What up doe? I go by Mina some call me Mimi. Damina Rose if you family. I don't care what you call me, call me shit just don't fuck with me. I'm a Highland Park Mich. born diva, HP being the mistress of Detroit in my eyes, in others it's just a crack whore to the pimp city. A little small fucked up city within a bigger fucked up city if you not really from the "D" then you probably don't know bout it and if you don't know you betta learn it aint shit to be played with. I'm 5'5 one hundred and twenty seven pounds, a nice voluptuous double D cup, twenty five inch waist blame it on the planks, and two big hands full of ass. I'm rocking a jet black at the bottom honey blonde then straight bleached at the top reaching an inch beneath my shoulders when its wearing its natural ringlet curl, with a milk chocolate complexion to compliment it all. I have two favorite features of myself one being my teeth they are straight, mine, and white perfect. Two would be my eyes no special color just dark brown but the way they were drawn, magnetic. I guess yawl can tell I love's me down boo.

Even though I was born up north well Mid-West to be exact I'm a Southern Bell at heart with Tampa all deep down in my soul. Why you ask, because it's the city that really molded me. A city I learned to use what I got and know, to get whatever it is that I want and need. My teacher if you will. Where I learned the saying, "The South is where it's at". A saying I learned was true. Now there aint nothing like up North now from the gritty music, original gangstas, home of the true soul music, crack heads, pimps and hoes, from the cold weather to the original hairdos and nails.

I love my metro Motown-Rock City in my eyes it's nothing realer. But you know we always want something on the side a down bitch, down south that's my down bitch. It's a different excitement a feel good vibe if you will the music the weather even style of dress it's just loud bright inviting. Seemed like in the south money never stopped I guess that's why the sun stays shining a little longer and no snow in sight so we can keep on moving and can't be slowed down, you know how us black folks hate snow and cold. Well I do if you don't. Yep the city that really molded me into who I am today. Highland Park gave me a steady foundation and Tampa planted on top of it. People that I know and known have said my life's a story, so here are a couple chapters. This story is my introduction facts and memories, you won't meet the present me till towards the very end just sit back and enjoy the ride.

In 1991 I came popping out my momma's lil coochie. Good shit happened in that year. Bill Clinton ran for office, Michael Jordan athlete of the year, Rodney King seeking justice, Evander retained his title, end of the cold war and I was coming out. I know the day of my birth to a T said she was out at Somerset South shopping, eating, she stayed busy. She felt pain but didn't want to miss any of the good new shit; she knew when all the new merchandise came into the stores. She was having a few pains but it aint phase her so she didn't stop, guess she wanted to literally drop. Pops was watching her from a distance like always and suggested they head home. On their way to the car my water bed broke and two hours later yes two hours later I have never been a lager. My mom and dad where sitting in the hospital bed watching "Candid Camera" and holding me.

My father was a man's man he came from dysfunctional family raised on the East side of Detroit always needing something or just plain wanting his parents to be there like they should be with their kids, involved. He always had to fend for self and his siblings. Having to grow up way ahead of time. A feeling he never wanted his children to feel, when and if he got to that part, a family, children most important. He vowed he would be there for them no questions asked because he knew the feeling of want, the feeling of need, and loneliness. He didn't want any of his seeds to ever feel how he felt at least not about him, their father. He also vowed he would keep the woman who bore his children her whole life. She wouldn't have a worry or care in the world but only if she allowed him to be there and play his part. He was a no nonsense man. He believed that his family was the most important thing in his existence. He was to protect, guide, love, teach and provide for us, his woman were to do nothing but be taken care of and be educated but of course if she wanted a career he would have no issues a woman being able to take care of hers if something happened to him was a plus. Even though my dad participated in the devils work that's what he called the drug game. He was really a gentle kind man we seen the side of him that nobody outside his family or even in his work circle would see. my dad stood six feet two inches blue black complexion and a presence that screamed to be noticed most importantly he was a man of his word, like he always say a "A man is only as strong as his word." That real man, Calvin Rose my dad.

Now my mother she was something else a feisty little thing royalty in the hood if you may. Her family was deep in the dope game her uncle was the top dawg and her dad was right under him. My mom lost her dad in the jail system and shortly after her mom disappeared in the jail system or so she thought she later found out her mom just ran off with a man and left her behind with her grandmother. Moms being the spoiled little girl she was and knowing her main source of income and shelter was gone she did what most ignorant kids do go find love and empty happiness in the streets. Fortunate for her my dad had her best interest at heart. He may have been older than her but with all the things she had seen and heard with her family's lifestyle she was a "G" a thorough breed someone who knew the rules and language of the game. She was crazy about him and that made it all the more easier. Mom's had the shape of a young Ertha Kitt the sex appeal of Dorothy Dandridge with the attitude of Foxy Brown at least that what she would tell me, she stood at a mere five feet three inches I thought she was beautiful, big round bright eyes a smile and laugh that light up a room and a walk that commanded attention. I don't think I ever seen her without heels on. I even heard she stepped in the hospital high stepping while I was preparing for my arrival. My mom the baddie DeAsha Rose.

Those two my mother and father were my hero's both of them, I looked up to my mom because she was what I thought a woman was posed to be she was beautiful smart and got whatever she wanted with no petty games or attacks. I looked up to my dad because he protected and loved us while providing everything we wanted and needed. A lot of the kids I knew didn't live with both their parents they knew and seen them both but to actually live with them and see them love and kiss on each other was a blessing for me. One that some of the kids and parents I'm sure had envy bout it deep down inside. Shit I did sometimes my mom would hog my daddy up.

Pops was a new freelancer contractor but had been doing his thing in the streets for years being that he didn't have his parents. At a young age he pretty much did what he had to do he started off as look out, to dealer, handling the block, to assign the blocks. The only thing about my pops is he had a number in his head he had a plan from the very beginning, since he been in the game since his single digit yrs. His plan was to make certain number then slowly back out and vanish not owing or needing anything. I guess he was determined to execute the plan when I came into the picture. My dad meet my mom when she was fourteen and he was seventeen she lied about her age telling him she was the same age as him with all the training of watching her mom and dad handle each other and to see how her mom carried herself it was instilled in her from the very jump how to be a lady of etiquette and appear mature. However she did tell the truth about her mom and dad how she came up and how they separated. She just didn't want to be turned away because of her age so she told a little fib. They dated for a yr. then I was conceived so you know mom had to tell her real age but my dad being who he is shook it off and continued to look out for his girl three years wasn't that bad they needed each other in his eyes. He would stay with her he just asked she graduated high school and she agreed.

Damn man… life. It's a trip. No matter how much we try and plan our course it never ends exactly how we want it. Man fairy tales, happily ever after, that shit is not real unless you writing a book. Life a game and we gamers, at least I am. I'm trying to play every day to get to the next level and I'm learning all the game codes along the way and fuck you if you not.

Netta B.

# Chapter Two

June 2002

Let's see, June 2002 don't remember the exact date but the day was Friday. The month and year is easy I guess it was a turning point mentally and emotionally. It's when I say when I kind of changed and woke up out of "it's your world" state of mind. It was one of those hot ass days this day in the hood one of those days that creep up from nowhere  the "D" had unpredictable weather fucked up is what pops liked to call it. It had been a pretty fun day though somebody turned on the fire hydrant like three house down and across the street. It started quiet till the kids blocks over heard about it next thing you know we had a full on block party. It was live from us kids running up and down the block to the parents ducked off enjoying their drinks and spliffs, dancing, talking shit yawl know what grown folks do.

The block was swollen people walking and cars creeping blasting music. It was cool everybody knew each other it was like a family affair. You saw guys with their Caesar cuts, nine fives a lot of fades. They were wearing Polo's, Louboutin, Sean Jeans, Chuck Taylors, air Jordan's, a few baseball caps. Rings on every finger or some with just a pinky ring, thick rope chains, Rolex or Cartier watches. You see the ladies with their doobie's, flat twist, bun ponytails, or micro's seen a lot of daisy dukes, miniskirts, ponchos, cut off shorts, Baby Phat, Enyce, Roca Wear, Bebe, a lot of summer dresses ladies was rocking gold big hoop earring bangles 3D motion rings and rocking shit like Adidas, Nike trainers, jellies or just some cute ass heels or flats. I was ten or eleven maybe I think my mom threw me on some cargo colored shorts a Cross Colours baby tee and some slides you know just some play gear. It was live I loved the summer time the heat whenever the weather decided to act right.

Our little block party lasted a couple hours before the fire truck came through and cut them shits off and everybody slowly made their way back to whichever way they came from. Some stayed behind mostly adults; it was Friday too these mugs was about to be out all night smoking and drinking good music and a lot of laughs and talking would echo through my windows. My mom sent me to get ready for bed soon as reached to open the screen door so I knew she was about to be sitting out front vibing too can't blame her though no fights, no police, a drama free day I didn't want it to end either. Earlier the adults planned on going to Belle isle Park tomorrow afternoon too so I was geeked, ready to get on that giant slide and run around the park like I was grown.

I was fresh out the shower settling in my room getting ready to watch Bernie Mac Show something me my mom's religiously did since TGIF stop coming on. I was working on my lil twelve inch TV. antennas just getting the picture right when my mom's boyfriend Corey came into my room told me my mom would be right back but he was there if I needed something which I didn't I just needed him out my eyesight "OK" I said he was about to walk off then asked me if I wanted a popsicle. You know I said yea I was tryna end my night right, just like them folks outside. Corey came back with mine and I guess one that was his. He gave me mine then sat and watched family matters a rerun that was on when that smooth and sexy Stefan Urquelle was on the scene.

Cal said he liked Urkel and wanted him to get Laura or some shit I wasn't really paying attention. While we were watching TV he turned around and said "let me see som..." before he even finished the sentence he stick his hand up under my night gown and grabbed my little coochie real hard the look in his eyes would scare anybody he was drunk on top of high his eyes were bloodshot and low with a strong smell of stale cigarette and weed smoke and a hint of crown royal on his breathe. I looked at him in shock, mainly because this nigga was real bold. What made his lil pea brain think he could just get away with something like this? I was trying to back up slowly so I could jet off I think this turned him on, a lil smirk came across his face as he pushed me back causing me to stumble and fall on my back at the foot of my bed. I tried to jump up but he already had me pinned with one hand and the other balled up in a fist clinched and ready to fall on my eye. "Lay yo ass back and don't say a motha fucken word. Or I will beat yo ass." Oh he was bold as hell for this shit I thought. I stared at his ass for a half of a second then I called his bluff. I started kicking, screaming, and going buck wild. That nigga had me fucked up thinking "I" was just gone lay and listen to everything like we baking cupcakes or some shit.

"My daddy gone get you" I yelled in between a useless attempt to break free.

"Yo daddy?" That nigga aint and can't do shit. How you gone tell him he hundreds of miles away, he don't care bout yawl."

Now that shit he just said got me heated I was going buck wild trying to get his hands off me I threw my white popsicle which is my favorite and I don't play bout food, ever. Oh he gone pay, my momma finna leave his ass we really moving to Florida or my daddy coming back either way this nigga done seen the last of us I was screaming in my head. "Stop touching me" I said in between my thoughts. I got a good knee kick in cause I heard him moan I don't know where I made contact but I was glad I did a lil damage. He was strong as hell though. He was holding both of my hands with one while trying to I guess touch and control my legs with the other. "My daddy gone fuck you up!" I yelled.

He looked up at me and smiled "Oh so you grown now, who you cussing at?" before I could give him a taste of the words I lost concentration because he lifted my night gown up still holding me down and stuck his rough stubbly face in between my legs rubbing he face hard in between my legs with both hands still occupied his left on the arms and right holding the legs. I kept screaming and attempting to kick and break free as much as I could I refuse to just lie still and quite. I knew what he was doing was wrong. But I also knew no one would hear me it was a party outside. He was so strong. I just began crying I didn't know what he was going to do and I didn't want to find out what kind of sick ass bastard fucks with a young child not even an adolescent all I could think about was Tammy this is how she felt I became more in-raged I wanted to kill him but he was just too strong for me. His mouth was now where his face was I was scared he was biting down there licking really hard pulling my underwear with his teeth. I thought he was done when he moved his face and one of his hands let me go, but it wasn't over he took his finger was trying to force it between my legs. My mom told me years ago don't nothing go down there that's my own personal private secret. I began bucking again swing my legs in any and every direction I could.

"Just be still I can't do it with you moving like this

you'll like it I promise." he kept rubbing in between my legs with his hand and I kept kicking and swinging I guess between my reaction and his slightly drunken state he wasn't going to fight with me, any longer. "Look you better get used to it, right now you don't like it but after a while you'll love it. I'm a turn two of the baddest woman in HP out" then he got up to leave mumbling shit under his breath "stupid ass little girl" he huffed and puffed grabbing in between his legs then turned and said "clean that popsicle mess up too before yo momma get back!"

Soon as both his feet touched the other side of my bedroom door I ran and locked it, walking to my bed in a zombie state. He called me a woman he really was sick and everything in his voice to his demeanor said he'll be back. After sitting on the bed for what felt like eternity but couldn't be any longer than a minute or two I felt scared up to hurt then way past angry and I wanted somebody to get Corey I picked up the phone and I dialed my daddies number.

"Hey Mimi I was just about to call you to say goodnight."

"Daddy Corey hurt me."

His mood quickly changed "What the fuck he do, yo momma let him hit you? He giving you whooping's now!?"

As I proceed to tell him what happen he was quite didn't say one thing just listened when I was done he was quite "Daddy, are you there?"

"Let me speak to your mother" I told him she wasn't there he asked where Corey was when I went in the living I seen Corey sleep on the couch. Nasty ass must of nutted and passed out I thought and my mom was now pulling up to the house I told my dad what was going on and when my mom came in I gave her the phone telling her it was my dad.

"Hey, how are you?" then it was quiet for a while my mom finally looked up at Corey then turned and looked at me. "I don't believe it." she said looking at me "I was gone not even 30 minutes Corey is here on the couch sleep and she sitting here she looks fine." she got quiet "I'll ask him about it she said. Yea whatever you don't have to call back I'll handle this matter of fact don't call my house again." She hung up. "COREY GET THE HELL UP" she screamed and kicked the side of the couch, he jumped up startled out of his sleep. "What did you do, TO MY BABY?!" she screamed and planted a nice knuckle sandwich to the temple this bought me momentarily happiness "What did you do to Mina you was touching on my baby feeling on her like a fucking pedophile?"

He started twisted his face all up looking disgusted "For real why would I wanna touch on that girl, a baby?!? I got you and you more than enough woman for me, I don't play with kids, get out my face with that shit you and that lying ass little girl."

I got the ass whipping of my life that night she told me don't fuck her relationships up just because I missed my daddy she wasn't trying to replace him or keep him away. That I needed to get over it cause Corey a good man and here to stay. I didn't say anything didn't try to make her believe me I just apologized then thought about how much I missed my dad and this very particular moment I needed him.

I remember the fight they had before pops told me he was moving. Man don't you hate it when everything is going so good and then something happens to fuck up your whole world it's usually when you talk to soon or think you can't be touched well my world changed the night I realized we wasn't gone be together forever we were going to split. One night while I was sleeping like the angel I was. Distress in the air brought me rite out my sleep and focused in on my mom and dad in the kitchen. I heard my dad voice who sounded irritated and my mom who sound like she was on the verge of a nervous breakdown.

"Well Calvin, damn do we have to, you can get out the game and stay here do we gotta leave the state just cause you wanna be clean?" she said sounding like she was pleading with him

"DeAsha look we gotta go. I would feel better knowing we all safe as family. I don't want to have to worry about anyone bothering you, Mimi, or me. I don't want to look over my shoulder cause a nigga tryna watch my every move or see what I got stashed up."

"But to Florida? Why Florida?"

"You know I hate this damn snow, slick ass streets, slick ass niggas, it's all the same the shit all of it will catch you off guard or possibly get you killed. I'm tryna go and it's for the better I'm not just thinking about me but us, come on you know this. We shouldn't even be having this discussion don't I always take care of yawl?"

"What about my family?"

"Come on D...yo family? Come on girl you barely see them except when they got they hand out."

"Well, what about my shop it's boomin I can't leave my clients like that."

"You own that, that money gone follow you wherever you go, talent gone always have clients you can build another round in Florida." my dad said sounding like he was hopping she gone say yes and stop with the bullshit, it got so quiet all but the heavy sound of my breathing. I stopped breathing just so I could hear every sound and movement that came from the kitchen I laid there wondering what their faces looked like were they standing or sitting. Then my mom broke the silence when I heard her say

"Well, what about Damina? All of her family and friends are here and she love Ford Elementary."

I couldn't believe she was putting me in this and if I knew my dad he couldn't either she, he, and I knew damn well I was a daddy's girl. I would go anywhere my daddy would lead and held on to his word like it was the bible itself, and thought my mom would too. I heard my dad take in a deep breath.

"D, you know I got family in Tampa and you know just like me she hate the cold and Florida got some good school systems down there way better than Highland Park and Detroit schools systems. We can put her in a magnet school so let's not go there." I heard some movements from the table and somebody open a can of pop and then my mom said the words that changed my feelings toward her. "You can go head, just gone n leave, but leave me and Mina out of it I'm not going and neither is she." After that it was silent no movements nothing I imaged my dad looking at my mom like *bitch is you crazy?*

"Word, nope, naw, fuck it I'm not leaving either yall my family we make moves together. Naw fuck it I stay here too." my dad said making me breathe a little bit easier but soon as it got better I tensed up again.

"Naw nigga gone ahead you need to go anyway I tired of you. You want to be a bitch get out the game and live off me and shit you probably don't got shit saved." that shit blew me away I couldn't believe what she had just said my feet were on the floor now "You probably owe somebody and you just running yea that sound like you Calvin tell the truth shame the devil you want us on the run with you. I mean we aint got shit to do with it. We safe me and my baby will be fine."

I couldn't believe what my ears were telling me it was pain in my heart so I'm sure it was murder to my dad. I didn't hear him say nothing I heard a big bang that sounded as if hands hit on top of the table a chair move and some footsteps and then the front door open and close. I sat there wondering if I should leave out my room and right when I was reaching for my bedroom door I heard sobbing my mother began to cry. I stopped dead in my tracks and got right back in bed as far as I was concerned she had no reason to cry she had just broken my dad's heart the man that took care of her and me made sure she had a way to survive if anything happened to him made sure we never wanted for anything and within a couple of minutes she took all the love time and energy he'd put out and striped it all from him told him she had no respect for him or his word. Loyalty was not being showed here and I knew my mom knew better maybe that's why she was in there bawling out of her big brown eyes. I knew that night my dad would no longer live with us he wouldn't let anyone disrespect him he fought to hard for it. I understood. I just went to sleep and prayed my dad made it back to me tomorrow.

Now those feelings that ran through me that night were back I felt hatred towards my mom she distrusted my dad and now she was turning on me. All through the night the phone rang sometimes she would pick it up then hang it right back up. I missed my daddy he believed me I hope he'd get through to her somebody needed to. She already sent my father away and now it looked like I would be next cause I be damned if I stuck around and endured another 2 seconds of that shit I was gone be a runaway or killa and I really hated the idea of leaving the comfort my house, so killa it was I thought as I drifted off to sleep.

Early that morning I heard my beeper vibrating it said 009-14 which read "hi boo" upside down. I really loved my dad and missed him I thought putting my beeper away. I wondered if he'd had talked to mom since last night, if Corey was gone. When I got up to see what was going on in the house I seen "Mr. new actor of the year" the anger scene award was still present. It basically was like nothing took place the night before. He was smiling mom was smiling and I was pissed.

Round one o'clock that afternoon while we were sitting at the table eating lunch before we made our way to Belle Isle we heard knock at the door which was strange we rarely got visitors. My mom sent me to go check it out and on the other side was my knight in shining armor I couldn't believe it my dad was there standing right in front of me. Every fear, doubt, uncertain thought and feeling I accumulated over the night was then lifted off of my shoulders. He smiled and hugged me hard making me feel safe. I was geeked since I knew him bout as good as I knew me I knew this was not going to be a pleasant trip this was definitely business. Daddy grabbed my hand and led me into the kitchen where we were eating guess he heard the sound of their voices. Mom's mouth dropped and Corey looked as if he was looking for a get a way. Dad looked my way then toward Corey and asked him to go outside sit on the steps with him "Let's talk and whatever else like real men do." When I looked over at Corey he was stuck looking like a goofball.

"Naw homeboy, here have a seat let's talk." He said matter factly with a giggle behind it.
"You just offered me a seat in a chair I paid for with that

table you're eating at in the house I bought for my girls and you offer me a seat? Nigga I own all this shit, if I want to sleep in the bed I will." he looked at mom and apologized I assumed it was for the ass whooping he was about to hand out and whatever damaged he would cause while giving it, meanwhile Corey was talking his mess.

"What up my dude, it don't even got be like this dawg...My bad my dude" he said now standing with his hands up.

"Yo bad?" pops grabbed a steel bat we had been keeping by the door in the kitchen since I can remember. "That sound like some shit a guilty nigga would say" he jammed Corey in the gut with the bat when Corey fell to his knees my dad landed a blow to the temple my mom hit him in the night before as well as the other temple also, I guess so it wouldn't feel left out. That's all it took to make Mr. Nasty take a quick nap. Pops was on a mission because he turned around stood dead in front and over my mother's tiny little frame and told her in all certainty with a calm and scary tone.

"How the fuck do you believe a bum over your own child? How you let her sleep under the same roof with a nigga that just violated her? How you whooping her when dis nigga doing wrong?"

"I thought she was jealous of him being here taking your place. I thou...."

"You thought, you thought. Bitch think about how I taking Mina ass with me." I went and jetted to my room still listening to every word.

"You can't just come..."

"Shut up! You don't get to make decisions regarding my baby anymore. Don't worry bout packing shit! We good as a matter a fact we gone leave now, gotta catch a flight" By the time those words fell from his lips I was standing next to him with my book bag and fanny pack ready.

Mom didn't say shit she just stood there looking kind of stupid. There were tears but one didn't fall yet. I guess she was trying to be strong not care, as we walked out the door I watched her, we met eyes for a second she waved and mouthed "I love you" then looked up at my dad she was looking at the back of him as he walked away. That's when the tears fell. I felt her pain she just forever lost a good man and possibly her daughter

We drove straight to Detroit Airport then straight on a plane for Florida. On the plane buckled in I was relieved I didn't have to do anything crazy my dad protected me and trusted me it gets no better than that. I respected him more than ever at that moment and I never would have thought that was possible. He must have felt me looking at him. He leaned over and said

"Getting joint custody was another preparation. I didn't want to think like this but if she ever messed up, abused her right as a parent in some way I would have the right to protect you."

By him saying that made me think of Tammy again. Tammy was my older cousin she mainly was my babysitter nobody but her watched me, it was always her. Dad working hard to get out the game and my mom working at the shop full-time Tammy was around a lot looking after me and I didn't mind at all. Tam was cool she respected me and I respected her. She treated me like a sister she taught, shared, and genuinely loved me. I found out the reason she lived with auntie was because her mother's half-brother was molesting her we were watching a movie and she just blurted out "Anybody touch you in a way that makes you feel uncomfortable tell somebody. Your best bet will be to tell your dad. I personally know how deep his love and protection goes, he dealt with my mom and her half-brother." That's all she said and I guess it's all she needed to say because it stuck with me. And in the end it proved to be true.

Netta B.

# Chapter Three

October 2002

Now when I tell you moving to Florida was a change the air was different, the trees were built different, and the sand you could find in random places in the middle of the city. It was the first time I ever seen someone with dreads. There were long ones, skinny ones, a couple big fat ones; even tiny one's just sticking every direction on the head. The thing that really got me was the gold teeth it seemed like everybody had them even saw a kid with some silver on two teeth. When they talk they're so country and I don't care what nobody say all "black" Floridians say "bike" instead of "back" and skr instead of str, and the darkest person love to throw on the brightest colors they can find which in the end somehow goes.

I was feeling it from the very beginning Mr. Rose was right. I didn't need to pack because I was gone need a whole new wardrobe out here. It was Hillsborough

County Brandon FL to be exact. Where my daddy stayed in the Brandon area we had flamingos, rabbits, ducks, and some kind of bird looking like a hungry ostrich in our yards absolutely nothing like Mich. all I ever seen there was rats, bats and roaches and you had to catch them at night most of the time and maybe a Red Robin or Blue Jay may have flown your way through the day but that was about it. The only time I seen strange birds was on TV or when I was at Belle Isle not in my yard Chilin, it was just a different experience and I actually liked it. Tampa was live, like on another planet being from Detroit. Music has always been in my heart Motown all day, and coming to Tampa expanded that they had some real booty shaking get up and vibe music. They had beaches all around and most importantly no snow I absolutely loved this scenery wish mom would have had her mind right to enjoy this life.

I had one friend Jennifer she was my dad's new homeboy daughter she was two years older than me but we were bout on the same page in life thanks to Tammy and I guess it's an only child thing we grow up a little fast being we are learning from all adults and their adult situations. Jennifer was white and Rican pretty girl they lived down the street just her and her pops but she was always with her sidekick a lil black skinny boy with dreads. His name was Javon he was a year older than me but they were in the same grade. Javon skipped a grade. They were in the 9th I was 7th it didn't matter doe we were thick as thieves most of their friends thought I was home schooled or went to some alternative school. I guess it didn't occur to them that I was just young, which I really didn't give a fuck, just leave me alone.

We pretty much hung out all the time we rode the hell out our bikes. Jen be like let's go let's ride get the hell outta dodge while it's still early. She loved to go she loved riding off whenever she could. We went to the candy lady house like every day I love them pineapple freeze cups soon as she went inside to go pick and choose them we would hit the candy lady up, a now and later here a hot sausage there whenever we got the chance I mean what kid didn't hit up the candy lady she had all the money anyway she wasn't hurting. Soon as whoever was inside throwing the goods outside foot hit the doorstep we would haul tail laughing and shit Jen be the first one to tell us "OK chill, tha fuck yawl still running for? Her fat ass is not gone chase us and we'd laugh while fucking them flip freeze cups up. I don't remember a candy lady in the "D" I knew the penny candy or corner store though.

Jen picked up where Tammy left and really taught me how to really interact with these little boys. That's all they are even when they grown-up well some not all. Back in the day me and Tam was walking to the store one of them days I didn't make it to the shop. I was probably bout six or seven Tammy was fourteen in the ninth grade. She was seven years older than me she was cool she was in school. My dad would hit her off with a couple dubs to look after me she stayed in East Pointe with somebody that was on her other side of the family she was cool a little lady, respectful, didn't talk too much shit I think that's why my dad let her come around me he thought she was a good influence and I agreed. While walking to the corner store on some random day, you know how young niggas in the hood get when they see someone different or new they act stupid.

"Hey what's up baby what's your name, where you going?" he yelled from the other side of the street, smiling either feeling good about himself or trying to give sex appeal.

"Not in the mood today" she said under her breath while grabbing my hand and kept walking head high.

"You little siddity bitch you hear me talking to you and you aint even all of that, rat looking ass." Cuz just rolled her eyes "Come on cuzzo" she said when we got into the store she said "Mimi don't talk to nobody that yells at you from across the street that nigga don't like you he is not interested he doing it for show and if he quick to throw an insult at you not even 5 seconds after throwing you a compliment that right there verifies what I just said his feelings hurt and he embarrassed all because he didn't act like a man and do it right in the beginning. Remember you get what you put out. This would be one of Unk's memory cap quotes so member that even if he don't tell you it, member that I did you deserve the best." I listened good and hard because like I did my mom I looked up to Tammy and just then she gave more reason to. She put something in my head to remember to put in use towards my life.

"Damn she THICK" one of the boys at the gas pump said about a girl walking by back to her car from the store, the girl smiled, and I think that threw my cousin over her limit.

"See Mimi that's probably all that girl needed to hear to believe all type of shit them bum ass niggas sellin done probably took some other girls pride goals and dreams and don't even know it. Now he on the next, don't fall for no man lesser than your dad. Uncle C is a great man it don't get no better than that a real man communicates, provides, and most importantly loves. He knows his role and he know shit hard and take time so he is full of patience. When I look for a man I compare em to Uncle C and even ask if he can meet them check them let em know somebody out here checking for me and know my worth. Another memory cap moment." she said with a wink. Tammy taught me how to pick them. Jen taught me how to play em. From both of them I learned the key was to be girlie, sharp, on your toes and ignore they ass and they came running everybody want something they can't have, it is amazing.

Jen was cool as fuck but some days I would see her and then the next day her dad would tell me she was sick wasn't feeling well must of been something she ate he would say. I just didn't get it she always looked and acted perfectly fine when I left her. I'd ask Javon how he felt and why he think she always disappearing and he would just blow me off like I aint say shit or just say what you asking me that for you know I want to see Jen today just like you. Javon and Jen was real close I think she had been playing that act like you don't like em card on Javon cause I knew for fact that he was open for her, at least that's how it seemed. On the days she was MIA we just got to the park or ride or bikes till our legs were ready to fall off it felt strange when she wasn't there she was like the glue the reason Javon and I even talked but hey everything happens for a reason he was the only young man I knew I may need him one day or he may need me. Either way I was holding on to him. Like my daddy I liked to keep my circle smooth and small.

One day when Jen didn't show up for school we began walking from school to Jen's we were geeked laughing and talking about a fight we seen on the route home between a gay boy and straight boy. The sissy drug that man up and down the street. Man I knew Javon was finna act this fight all the way through I just knew I was finna die laughing. The fight was funny as hell I mean it's beyond true when they say "Don't judge a book by its cover" I mean you could miss a lot and set yourself up for failure. Any way that had to be the funniest fight I ever seen. We couldn't wait to see Jen. Javon jetted off "Last gotta kiss ass" he said cracking up getting ready to turn the corner we knew she would be out on the porch waiting. As soon as we hit my block we seen the police cars all in front of the house it was three of them 5-0 was walking around the house and talking to Mr. J who was sitting outside on the porch looking lost and hurt at the same time. We walked to my porch sat waited and watched to see what was going to happen next to see if Jen was going to come out or something.

Javon sat at the bottom of the step just watching not saying anything didn't even move. I wasn't sure what was going on but by the way Javon looked I knew something wasn't right and it had something to do with Jen. I didn't say anything didn't even want to ask him if he need or wanted something was scared he might of snapped so I went in for a drink maybe he'd follow me in, he didn't. When I finally made my way back out the door the last uniform there was the one who was talking to him when we first walked up, he was shaking Mr. J's hand after that he got in car and left Mr. J looked at us head down hands in pockets then walked in the house. Javon sat for about a min then left didn't say nothing just got up and walked off which then turned into a run. I just sat and thought what was going on. I hope Jen felt better tomorrow because I needed some answers of what was going on was there a burglar loose was she sick is it cancer was it sickle cell, I needed to know.

PRETTY: Her Introduction

# Chapter Four

December 2002

It had been weeks since me Javon seen the police at Jens house and I still hadn't seen Jen, Mr. J, or Javon for that matter and I was feeling down I needed my BFF's I just left my soccer game, the season just started and we won. I wanted to celebrate with my homies but they were out of reach my dad's contracting business was booming and I wasn't seeing a whole lot of him but I knew at the end of the day he had my back and would always be there. Leaving the park where we had our game I put on my head phones and started heading home I lived bout three blocks from the park. Walking through the lot I spotted Mr. J's truck I practically broke out in a sprint tryna get to the truck I just knew Jen would be in there or on her way to it when I got to it Mr. J was there looking a hot mess.

"Hey Mr. J. how you been? Where Jen at have you heard anything?" I asked him standing on the driver's side door panel peeking in the back seat.

"We still don't know"

"So did she run away or did someone kidnap her"

"I don't know. She was there then she was just gone. A little blood was found on the floor but that's it just a spot, no trail, nothing broken, no finger prints. "Nothing"

"It's OK, I'm sure we'll see her again. She's strong."

"I hope so I miss my baby, she was the only one I had to take care of me, and I…." He busted into tears.

"Don't cry, be strong she'll be back" I gave him a reassuring hug threw the window "Your just like my dad a good dad, Jen never said anything bad about you she has no reason to run away, and too strong to stay locked up. She'll be back." I tried to assured him."

I guess he appreciated it and I made him think of my dad because he said "Come on your dad sent me out here to get you."

This was some excellent news music to my ears cause my calf's, hamstrings, shit my whole body was aching so I was happy to oblige no questions asked. I ran my happy ass to the other side and hoped in the truck I needed this ride I didn't feel like walking and being back in the ford made me think of Jen we'd shared so many secrets and stories in this back seat just laughing and giggling.

"Dang I really miss her so, can't wait till she come back." I said looking in that back seat.

"You just don't know how much" he said stopping and turning to face me looking confused like he was about to say something deep a mind blowing thought then he smiled. "I miss her too but at least I got you around to help me remember her" he said with an almost sinister look on his face. That look gave me chills and lump in my throat before I could comprehend to make a move he reached up and grabbed at my shirt. *Oh no not again.* I thought, *who can I tell now this time it's daddy's friend will he believe me?* He pulled at my soccer shorts. *Will he say I deserved it or I must be asking for it?*" Do you want a real daddy?" he asked me.

"I got a real fucking daddy, get off me"

"Calm that shit down. I'll kill your ass nobody know we together." he said

"You said my da..."

"I lied." he said holding a pocket knife out. "Shut up

don't move or I will cut your ass up" he pulled my shorts and panties down just above my knees. "Now lean back." I did as I was told and I cried because it was happening again. *Why does this shit keep happening to me!? What the fuck, is a sign gullible little girl written on my fore head? How the fuck I'm a get out of this I broke one of my dad's rules for me.* **DON'T TRUST NOONE.** Now I had to rep the consequence of not listening. In one quick move Mr. J had done what I escaped from in Detroit. His hand was clenched around my neck while the other held the knife. He panted like dog and the sweat from his face and body dripped on me. I even think he called me Jennifer. The knife was no longer in his hand because it know trying to penetrate my vagina he started with two but later proceeded with one making its way inside my body. I was terrified thoughts ran through my head. I don't know what he said I was too busy screaming hoping somebody would ride by or walk by. No one came to my rescue. As I kicked and screamed he continued to clinch my neck. He backed off looked at me and said. "I would of thought your cherry would have been picked already. Guess somebodies dad isn't as smart as me. I got to pull my pants all the way down for this." he said with a sinister laugh. With his hot breathe he whispered in my ear "It's too good I can already tell." He began tugging at his pants but was having a problem with his belt and he sat the knife on the floor board *shouldn't have done that dummy; I may be tired but you holding me down with one hand.* I thought to myself. He went for his pants to unbuckle them I pulled one hand free kicked him between his legs and swung the knife as fast I could as many times as I could while I reached for the door and fell out his truck onto my back in the gravel. I pulled my shorts up gripping the knife like it was my air then spun around and ran.

"You little bitch! You cut me!" is all I heard before I ran through the park in route to my house something made me stop in my tracks and turn and say

"Yea well you got off easy. I hope you bleed to death and if you don't every time you see that scare you'll think of me...oh and if I see you again I'll kill you." I don't know why I said that last part but I really felt like I meant it.

I was so happy to be running, to be away from him and his beady lil eyes and sweaty shaking hands, pale white skin ugh the thought of him touching me I wanted to stop and puke. I ran for my life through the field in between homes to the streets, not wanting to stop till I got to hood, my street, my environment, my home. The whole time I ran, a remixed chopped and screwed version played itself throughout my head. I heard the panting and heavy breathing he pushed in my ears so clearly. A sound I'm sure I would never forget along with a feeling attached.

I hope he was still there because I was about to send an army out to get his white ass. I trusted him and he took my kindness for weakness what was I thinking to go with him to think he was my friend why would he want to be my friend I was just a little girl and he was a man a grown man I had no business. I can't tell anybody. What would I say? I would go home and act as if nothing happened. One day he'll get his. I don't know if it will be under my hands or the lords but he will get his. I Thank you lord for this day and the sway of my feet. I prayed.

That night was the night that I was not only in shock yet again but enraged. I busted in my house and just sat right on the couch and didn't move. I dropped everything or left everything in Mr. J truck or on the ground where ever it fell my soccer shorts where ripped I lost one of my shin guards left my cleats along with my school bags. I sat there and wondered how I would tell my dad about what happened and most importantly how I would tell on his only friend this was hard. But because of what happened tonight I was sure Jen ran away or Mr. J did something to her and he was probably feeling all on her beating her or something why else would she be there then the next day she'd be gone. It was all starting to make since why she really said not only nothing bad about him but nothing about him at all. Probably why she was so outspoken and soothing at the same time, she not scared of nothing but she knows what it feels like to be scared maybe she was fighting back more and more and she was getting bruised up that's why we hadn't seen her in a while. I had to figure it out next time I see Javon we would have to talk whether he wanted to or not.

When dad came home I was still in the same spot two and half hours later but sleep. He woke me up and asked was I OK "Rough game Mimi? You look like you been through It." he laughed. I just hugged him and cried "It's OK Mimi we lose some it gives us character and makes us stronger. I bout you some food from Leroy Selmons go wash up and come eat." I couldn't even bring myself to tell him so I got up washed up and came back down stairs with a story in mind.

I told him I got jumped after the game and they stole my school bag cleats and stuff. I guess they don't like winners I egged it on a group of jealous girls and they seem like they were older than me too.

"Girls will be girls just show them how it's really done. Be thorough be direct don't let no one run over you let them know you are not to reckoned with by actions doings and with very few words and you won't have to get physical violent do you understand"

"Yes, sir" and I did.

Netta B.

# Chapter Five

January 2003

Javon finally started coming back around and Mr. J just vanished maybe he did bleed to death or was just scared my dad was gone kill his ass. Somewhere running scared I hope. He damn well deserved it for my girl Jen me and whoever else. My dad didn't really notice it he was too busy working on the job and his little hoes, shit he figured he just needed to get away and go back home grieve for his child.

I was just so happy my soup for my soul was back. I don't know why he was acting all funny anyway we were cool we could get through this together. He finally up and told me he was real hurt about Jen leaving and he had to deal with it in his own way and time. Said he knew for a while now that Jen dad was doing things to her and he knew that's the reason why she left. She would always say one of these days. He didn't know what she meant exactly like if she was gone kill him one of these days or just run away. But on that day Jen disappeared he realized what he already he knew and it hit him hard and he just needed time and I now knew why he was looking the way he was that day on my porch because he didn't know if she was hurt or if she dipped. But I guessed he figured it out by the end of the meeting between twelve and Mr. J that's why he left the way he did his heart was broken.

"I just can't stand Julius and he would get what he deserved one of these days." Javon busted out of thin air and I felt the rage and pain that he felt, and somehow I felt closer to him. I was relieved he expressed the way he felt. I was feeling like I could trust Von. I asked him if he wanted to take a walk, he agreed and I told him my little story about my dad moving out here to how he came to my rescue and brought me out here and then told him what Julius did by time I told my whole little life story I was so angry and hurt not only for me but for Jennifer too, in the mist of passion I blurted out how I could kill them niggas. I really wanted to, they both was bold for that and people like em who do harm for no reason but personal gratification should be offed I wish I had skills to do it. I looked up at him just knowing he was looking at me like I lost my mind just ready to call me crazy or some shit but he was actually there listening deep and hard like he knew a way like it was possible. He took a deep breath looked up at me dead in my eyes.

"Yea shit crazy out here. I'm sorry you had to go through that. I got your back for as long as I'm living."
He sounded nonchalant as hell, but the fact that he said it and was looking at me straight in my eyes. Those facts alone made me believe and trust it. We became real close after that. Von stayed with his uncle who was a mechanic and cleaner. Weird I know, both jobs I would think was full-time jobs but shit whatever can't knock a man's hustle. Von lived with his uncle because both of his parents died in a car accident coming from dinner when he was eight. It made me realize why he was so serious so sincere he knew the meaning of one day you here the next you can be gone and experienced not just once but twice.

His uncle was cool stayed out in Riverview in a big house had two blue nose pits and a white girl who looked like a playboy bunny. Real cool ass slick man didn't put me in the mind of a mechanic or cleaner he always stayed fresh clean footwork, nice cut, smelled delicious, and nails clean as a Monte Carlo. He didn't look like no 9 to 5 worker but more like the Nicki Barns kind as far as I was concerned. Maybe it was some shit he told Von so he wouldn't follow in his footsteps probably something he promised his-self or maybe to Von's parents. He could be fooling Von but he aint fooling me or shit maybe they both was fooling me. I'll let them think that, I didn't care I was a little girl in their eyes they don't know my pops use to run shit out in the "D" and I got a memory cap full of streets on phonics.

I'd play the game I loved coming over here Unk let us go in the back shoot guns, throw darts, put the boxing gloves on, man they let a lady let her hair down back there. It all started with me asking about a gun I saw sitting on the back porch in broad daylight and after that it was a wrap. He started us off with bb guns and then it went to real guns like a Ruger Revolver which fit in my hand perfectly. I was good at shooting almost like throwing a ball almost every time I hit bulls eye must have been those duck hunt games on Nintendo. We went fishing which turned out to be relaxing Von taught me how to meditate out there in the middle of the water. I even learned how to play chess which is real easy just remember the pieces their place and movement it's a piece of cake...right? I love the game. Unk was real cool you had to give him that. I found out that he let Javon drive. Javon was only thirteen but hey I guess he would be fourteen soon but damn he was lucky, over here shooting fishing driving and shit. My only question is why me him and Jen aint been did this shit she could have maybe put one in Mr. J big ass head.

\*\*\*\*\*

My personal life was going great I had my bestie, me and dad still on point with each other never missing a beat. I spoke to my mom a lot she was still doing her thing out in the "D" asking me to come up soon and I was thinking it would be one summer definitely not the winter or fall. I was cool I loved my new environment I really didn't have no desire to go back to Detroit if I wouldn't have heard the conversation between her and dad or if she wouldn't have picked dick over blood, her own creation I probably would've been back by now but shit I'm like her, fuck it.

One evening while doing our regular daddy daughter time we were watching Uptown Saturday Night with Bill Cosby and Sidney Poitier. One of our favorite movies since I can remember when heavy knocking at the door distracted us. And they were serious about somebody answering.

"Yea, hold the fuck on, shit!" I looked up over the couch I felt just like how my dad was feeling right about now. *Who the fuck was ruining daddy daughter time?* I thought still looking over my shoulder. My daddy swung the door open to a pretty yellow complexion Sanaa Lathan looking chick with a back in the day Toni Braxton haircut, holding a freakin baby. This bitch finna get cussed out I thought her goofy ass at the wrong house and shit ringing the bell all wild.

"Hey Calvin." she said with much attitude my dad was looking stupid. "You gone let me in or what? Damn." *No!* I thought waiting for my dad to tell her ass to "Get-ta steppin" like Martin would say.

"What's happening?" my dad managed to get out I turned completely around now faced front and center now tucking my knees up under me arms propped on the back of the couch, I tryna get some understanding of what was going on. My dad looked shocked and confused and she looked distraught worried and scared. She bit on her lip looked behind her then at the baby in her arms and back up to my dad.

"Look I need you to take this baby"

"What! I already got a baby!" he said looking at me. She looked too and the sight of me sitting there looking dead at her with questioning eyes and eyebrows may have startled her but also pushed her to get out what she had to say.

"Well now she has a brother." She said matter factly.

"Plus you got a man remember that's why you left me. I aint seen or heard from you in like ten eleven months and now you tryna give me a baby talking about I'm the daddy, seriously now, this aint happening." My dad said finally getting his swagger back.

"I know, but I cheated with you and only you, you the daddy, look at him he almost a month and you can already see you. Get a DNA test if you don't believe me." she sounded as if she was pleading. My dad looked at the baby and started shaking his head that made her bout break down.

"Look I'm not putting my baby up for adoption, aint no telling where he'll end up I don't want child support, shit, I'll pay you child support. I just want you to take care of our baby and give me an occasional update. No strings attached."

"Well why did it take so long for you to tell me or bring the baby here if it is mine." dad inquired.

"I wasn't sure who the father was, I was cheating. I didn't want to tell my man I might have another man's child in my belly. When he came out we seen the color you know my dudes white he was furious flew out the delivery room he tried at first to coup with it but couldn't he said he is not raising nobody else's child and I couldn't blame him he shouldn't have to I was wrong. I know my baby Calvin Jr. will be safe with you if you can raise a beautiful daughter a boy should be a piece of cake. she handed little Calvin to him then I heard a horn blow she tighten up said thank you waved at me and kissed little Calvin and told my dad I love you but I'm in love with him. I'll be in contact." She jetted out the front door and to her Bentley.

PRETTY: Her Introduction

# Chapter Six

May 2003

I loved having our little Cal around it was pretty fun till he cried and shitted but other than that I couldn't wait till this little thing started crawling walking talking shit or something. I stayed at the crib and helped as much as I could and daddy hired some workers to handle the business for his contracting business work. This new found family back at three was great but I needed to get out so I got up with Javon and Unk I needed to go fishing. Fishing was exactly what I needed peace and quiet but I would hold on to the quiet part cause I had so many questions for Unk.

"How long had been a mechanic and why are you never at work?"

"Why are you always on point? You remember everything, you see everything, you good at planning and move silently and smooth. I began to get a little uneasy and shift in my seat Unk caught on "I'm sorry don't tense up it's OK." he looked at Von an asked if he was OK he replied "Yea, waiting for a bite." He turned back around thought for a second.

"Javon told me you want to be a mechanic."
I looked at Javon who looked at me. "What you looking at girl? Unk talking not Me." he said laughing.

"No offense but I'm a lady. I aint tryna be all up under a car getting dirty.

He chuckled "Me neither."

I knew it was some other shit going on so his statement didn't confuse me but made me very curious "Well what exactly do you do as a mechanic. I may want to be one. I see how you're living seems pretty stress free."

"I get rid of the expired when your time is up I take you out of your misery, and clean you on up."

"So you a doctor?"

"I don't heal I kill." I sat there looking at him waiting for him to say something else like sike or some shit but he didn't so I chimed in

"That's what I thought, so you are like Samuel Jackson and John Travolta in Pulp Fiction or like Daddy Cool the book by Donald Goines."

"Oh snap what you know about Donald Goines?"

"I know D.G. done read most of his books he from the "D" I have an interest in things and people from my hood so am I rite are you a hitman"

"Yea, I guess you can say that I'm a hit man, but I prefer cleaner, I just like the way that sounds bet..."

"Yes sir that's what I want to do." I interrupted he sat there looking at me with a straight face and I didn't flinch.

"Then you shall be. I'm a train you I don't think it'll take long at all with you. You're a person with excellent motor skills communication skills great focus and determination. You gone be a force to be reckon with. Believe me."

I went home that night on top of the world I knew it was a reason for Javon I'm a be a fucking hit woman I 'ma get those two little miserable bastards that think it's OK to touch on little girls and shit. I can protect my family and myself. Unk was rite I will be a force to be reckon with I pity the fool. What would be my mark my signature what would be my name so many decisions I was so excited. How will I find those bastards mom dumped Corey whack ass it took my dad taking me away for her to open her eyes up though so sad it shouldn't even had gone there to be honest. How would I get my hands on Mr. J he just disappeared into thin air another fucking loser oh well they'll get theirs one by one little by little even if it's not by me it's in the cards. They played a fucked hand so they get fucked results.

My first few days training was kind of boring I don't know if it's because I'm a freaking child or because he was really checking my patience but obviously I passed his little test it was a lot of chess, archery, learning all eleven pressure points, some meditation, blind folded exercise, cardio, and a lot of exercise and weights. The meditation was my favorite one I did it a lot It was calming I could relax anywhere but still be focused on everything you know how they say if you are without a sense all of your other senses become a little bit more magnified well that was definitely true. With my eyes close I smelled and heard a thousand times better. I used this little trick every change I got, when in school I would just close my eyes while in class and pick up on people whispering, hear doors shut and heels clicking in the hallway. It's amazing how you don't even know the things you can do or could have done until it's taken away or brought to your attention. We even used Javon as a target sometimes I scared the shit out of J so many times he aint see hear or smell me coming.

May 2005

Over about a course of two years with me training with Unk Javon and I had gotten even closer he was now looking at me the way I seen him look at Jen but without the pity and worry. One day after my training session while Von was walking me home he began talking to me. "When you told me you were mad and wanted revenge on those men that violated you and the ones close to you I believed you and sensed you could really do it. You came around me and Jen you were younger than us but you were also smarter than us street wise you knew what was what and I respected it then and now. I know you still young, focused on something and not even looking at boys yet but I need you to know when you do begin I'm a be rite here waiting. When I said I got your back as long as I'm living I meant it you gone be my wifey I'm not saying you got to be my girl now or tomorrow. I may not even be what you want right now but someday you will, you gone see exactly what it is and feel how I feel. I love you girl I know you only thirteen but you smart and if you any kin to your dad you got all the sense." He kissed me on my forehead then continued to walk the route to my house.

My mom was 15 and just completed her sophomore year when she had me and I was not taking the same route no matter how fine, smart, tempting this boy was. I was shocked I couldn't believe what had just taken place someone just told me they love me beside family and I think he really meant it. I started showing my love for him too, but with subtle moves. Lingering in on a hug, a glance that last two seconds longer than usual, or something as simple as a touch things I seen my mom and dad do so I knew they had to be real signs of affection.

Unk caught on to the shenanigans one day while we

were playing chess he caught me off guard with a slew of questions. "So what's up with you and nephew?"

"Nothing we still cool just been training with you or watching my little brother I don't get to see him as much." I said hopping to throw him off guard

"Oh yea you are clever, but answer my question." he said not fazed by my answer one bit

"If I answer your question you gotta answer two of mine."

"Damn two?"

"Yea, it's a two part question plus you might run back to J and tell him what I said so it just evens out if you answer two."

"OK" he said I put my little thin hand over the glass chest board looking to shake hands. He shook it I answered

"I love J he gone be my baby daddy" I said taking his little pawn. He thought that was o so funny he laughed deep from within at that one but I was so serious I already knew J felt the same that's why I said it. I laughed too because just to see him filled with glee put a smile on my face. When he died down I went in with my question.

"What's your mechanic name?"

"Pieces"

"Why did you pick that?"

"Every time I off someone I take a piece, before I kill em" he said smiling.

"A piece of what?" I said side eying him

"Of whatever I want. An ear, finger, eye, nail, tooth whatever I feel like." Thank god it was body parts and not a piece of ass I thought.

"So why you do that?"

"Every mechanic has a signature whether it's the method of the killing, what's before during or after the killing like Daddy Cool his thing was knives. You should think of what yours will be your name and signature."

"I want a name like Whisper, Silent, or Quick like off Harlem Nights and I want to do whatever method pops to mind for that target the best way to get them I want to leave my options open whether it messy or spotless. No limits here." Unk laughed again. I was just tickling his little fancy today. I know he wasn't laughing at me, but with me, I know kids say the darnedest things.

Netta B.

# Chapter Seven

August 2005

It was my fourteenth birthday my mom had come down to Tampa to see me and I was kind of krunk about it I aint seen her since my dad rescued me. I was worried to see how they would interact even if she would say she wanted to stay with us or even how she would take lil C cause I grew to love him he would be three soon which was cool because I was over the terrible twos phase.

We drove to Tampa airport to go get mom maybe a thirty minute drive. It was nice out a cool low 80's wind blowing sun shining, and the interstate was wide open no traffic and airport traffic was flowing like water. While we were sitting by the baggage claim daddy peeped her first. "Look there she go." with a *Damn!* Right after under his breath. I knew she was the only woman my dad ever loved I knew then but I could see it plain as day now.

I couldn't even blame pops doe my momma was looking good she put on some weight probably like ten pounds but it was all evenly distributed the weight all put her probably in the 135 area so not bad she got a short cut now I was shocked to see all that long hair gone. I was never cutting mine, it would fall to my feet and I'd be literally tripping all over it before I cut it that short unless I'm on the run. Anyway we watched her wait for her bag and look over her shoulder and back to her watch a couple of times probably cussing us in her head. I seen some dreads try and grab her hand one white guy ask her something she shook her head and he walked off I guess that was the straw for daddy no more lurking time to go get his woman or ex woman shall I say. Which I'm surprise she aint peep us earlier with lil C loud hyperactive self.

"Lola" my dad said as he crept behind mom she turned around with the biggest smile I ever seen that I had to smile too at the reminiscent name. Pops use to call her Lola because of some song talking bout whatever Lola want Lola get or some shit, typical spoiled brat song. She gave him a hug then hugged me tight saying my old school name "Hey Ladybug" that made me smile but it was soon gone I was happy to see her but felt some type of way. All of a sudden I had a feeling wishing this was us dropping her ass off at the airport. She seen lil C after my hug I had a tight grip on his little hand if I were to let it go I'd be chasing his little fast tail up and down this airport he was definitely a track star in training. He wanted a hug too he seen me and dad get one now it was his turn mom thought it was so cute she picked him up and played with him while we waited for her bags.

"So how have you been" she asked dad

"I've been good I really can't complain I got 2 little munchkins that keep me young, busy, and in my bank account." he said laughing "How's the shop?"

"The shops still running smoothly I spend most of my days in there I am single so I have tons of time to stay in the shop which is a blessing. I thank him constantly for placing you in my life and actually caring enough. Thank you Calvin..." She looked over at me then back to lil C "Damina you need to come and check it out see how you may want to run the business because it's going to be yours soon, and plus I miss my little diva. And if you don't come I might have to kidnap lil C here he is so cute." we laughed and joked about how she aint got to steal just let us know how long he'll be gone well pack his bags. She thought that was so funny.

Once we got her bags we went to Channel Side and went to bowl a little ate a little and caught up some more. We learned mom kicked Corey out the day dad beat his ass and brought me to live with him. She took her time took all the blame and explained how she actually believe Corey and thought I was just latching out because I missed my dad and wanting some attention a way for pops to move back to Mich. It wasn't till dad came to kick some ass that she realize that I was telling the truth she saw the apologetic and scared little boy in Corey that day and felt horrible after we left she called up rocky one of dads right hand homeboy in Detroit he called up Nookie his brother and they removed Corey from the house she hadn't seen or heard from him since that day so she couldn't really say what he up to now a days. She said she went through a depression she lost two of the most important and only people she had in her life. Her very own family and pushed them both away because she was scared of change.

When she said that I think it did a lot for me and dad because I think it was something we both needed and wanted to hear from her and it was such a relief to hear it and early in her visit now I was actually happy she was here and about to spend my fourteenth birthday with me. It had been a long time and it was well over due.

The day of my party I guess moms will be moms, because she pulled me over to the side during the party to have a mother daughter moment weird timing but whatever.

"So Mina how have you been what's going on with

you?" before I could say anything she cut me off "And when I say that I mean school your about to be a freshman in less than a month are you going to try out for sports, star in theater, do you plan on going to college are you coming back to Detroit?"

I didn't know what to say all I'd been thinking about was killing me a mutha fucka aside from keeping my grades up I hadn't put too much thought in all that, I didn't need higher education I was gone be a millionaire 2 times over by time college came and in all honesty I don't want to go back to Detroit too cold and it stay gloomy looking on too many days. I just gave her the most mature close to honest answer I could muster. "Mom I'm so excited, I'm bout to meet a whole new group of people. I want to try out for cheer or dance team. I'm not sure what I'll do after school I haven't thought that far along, but I'll keep you posted." With that answer my mom appeared to be satisfied. She was on to bigger fish to fry.

"I see that you and Javon seem to have eyes for each other." She watched me shift in my seat a little before she continued. "I don't think you're having sex or anything. I just see you both. If your hearts in it you need no other reason just follow it." She caught me off guard with this so I asked her what she meant she looked up and straight ahead. When I seen what she had seen I smiled wide and big without even thinking about it.

"That right there if he makes you smile, and glow like that he's a keeper he already knows your family and he's your friend, two very important factors taken care of."

"Well how do you know if he likes me?"

"Mina I already peeped this whole scene he stay looking up for you seeing what you doing if you OK he bout as bad as your daddy was. Don't let your husband slip through your hands I'm not saying hurry up and make him your boyfriend because your still a little girl but just let it be known, mark your territory. Keep his interested piped and his friendship strong." She said then got up and sashayed her way over to where my dad, Unk and some of the fam were.

I sat there and let what she just said to me marinate it wasn't like she just said some profound shit it was just it had been so long since she sat and talked to me and shared it was like a memory cap moment. I really missed her just didn't know how to take her or if I could depend on her it would get there eventually though just not right now.

We did have so much fun on my birthday night we played so many games ate till we couldn't any more. While our parents drank and laughed me my cousins and Von snuck off on the roof a place I always hit up when I'm tryna "think" my little get away. We sat up there and blazed on a joint talking and laughing until the sky turned midnight then we finally saw the grown folks all outside talking they mess bout where we at and what we doing that's when we had to pop up on em like what up doe. Everybody was feeling good the parents and the jitts. Everybody slowly made their exits wishing me happy birthdays and many many more. People wishing my mom a safe flight back and hopefully she'd come back so they could see her again soon. Personally I loved my mom she was my mom but at the end of the day she hurt us both in the same way not having trust in us, and I was happy to be dropping her off tomorrow afternoon.

Before Unk pulled off he ran up to dad pulled him to the side and they got in a deep conversation meanwhile Javon had something on his mind he wanted to get out, he stepped out the car and grabbed my hand looking dead into my eyes.

"Mimi there is no turning back now you're getting what you wanted so bad to have a piece of..." My heart started beating so fast I was bout to get my first kiss or he was gone actually ask me to be his girl moms was rite I wonder if she said something to him tonight to aint no telling with her ass. He brought me out of my thoughts and back to reality. "Um Unk..." Why the fuck he talking bout Unk? "Unk said you ready you gone receive a letter priority mail tomorrow it's gone have my name on it but it's for you. I feel sorry for the people in your future they won't even see it coming."

"OMG my first target don't play with me Von"

"Your name is Pretty that's all they know on you that you go by Pretty."

"Pretty? What wait, why Pretty? Who thought of that, how can I make a dead target pretty? That does not even go. Dang, why I didn't have a say in the name mine was better."

"It's just a name girl, it don't define you baby. It's all good even though if it was based of looks it should be "Wifey" cause that's what you look like to me." At that moment in time I felt the biggest smile spread across my face and a little tingle I never felt before I must say I felt a little embarrassed at the same time but if his plan was to shut my ass up it definitely worked cause right at that moment I was speechless. "Your clients don't know your name, age, where you live not even your ethnic background. Instruction on everything will be in your priority mail. You got what you wanted so handle it go get to your retribution. I'm a talk to you later. I love you little ass girl, happy birthday."

I really wanted to kiss him but I knew I'd be stepping on some toes with that so I came back to earth said bye to him and Unk hugged my dad goodnight kissed my mom night and went back through the window and on the roof to think before I went to bed. I was now 14 with a new understanding with my mom, a profession that would make me a very wealthy woman and I had a man who understood what I did and why. I had it going on at a young age, now I just had to shape it and get my revenge. Why? Because what they did was and is unacceptable. Tomorrow would be a new chapter in my life, Chapter fourteen the beginning. All I had to do was get this money. Love my man and live.

The next day I was hawking looking for the mailman and when he came I jetted out the door got the mail for some reason I expected a box but it was just a manila size letter luckily the mail came while my dad was taking my mom to the airport so my dad wasn't there to ask no questions.

In the house I sat down on the couch me and little C. Now shit was about to get real. I thought, it's not the training stage anymore it's the get it done stage or I would be on somebodies hit list next. I grabbed the envelope and opened it, right then lil C grabbed at the paper which scared me a little and made me a little paranoid like he could read or some shit I was tripping he looked up at me like *Whateva* then went on to crawl off the couch and scoot to floor as to say you need some alone time. I just laughed at myself I was paranoid and didn't even start the killing yet. I laughed out loud lil C looked at me again like this girl going crazy. The coast was clear I tore it open it had a piece of paper an envelope and photo.

I picked up the picture first and looked it was a lady she looked like she was in high school. Pretty girl she was sitting at the beach looking up out in the sky looking very relaxed. I looked at her she was so pretty I wondered what she could have done then I remember sitting at home in the "D" watching the news with my dad something we did a lot of catching the evening news. He would say "I know it's bad and scary at times but you got to know what's going on around you." back in 2001 the trail of Derek and Alex king who killed their dad, they were just a few years older than me at the time, they seemed normal sound mind even spoke better than some adults I knew but were some bad seeds. You can't trust anybody sometimes not even yourself we are very emotional beings. Crime comes in different shapes, colors, and forms. I knew she had to be some type of sick-o I only wanted to deal with the folks that harmed children. I pulled out the paper that read target.

# Kimberlyn Jones
## Age: 17
## Race: Black and Korean
## Height: 5'7
## Weight: 142

## Address: 7839 Fern St
## Apollo Beach, FL. 36781

## Employment: Jet Ski and Thangs
## Hobbies: varsity basketball player, golf, swimming, skating, and arts
## Interest: performance arts, history, entertainment, and fashion

Kimberlyn Jones is a high school senior, no kids no siblings mom passed due to a bad kidney where she moved to live with father in Florida at the age of ten born in Teflon **GA.** the summer she moved to **FL.** her father began molesting her, she has molested young boys and girls at the age of 13 when she started her babysitting jobs. She was accused once two years ago by a young girl. Subject wants her gone she abused a seven year old boy continues sticking broom sticks up her vaginal region. She is said to have and sex addiction, **OCD,** and controlling. She works every Tuesday and Thursday afternoons every other Sunday.  She has no race, sex, or age preference

Expiration date: **NOW**
Completion call 8185555187 ext. 187

Netta B.

# Chapter Eight

Oh shit! A child a fucking kid? A fucking bully. I was kind of pissed I did not want to harm kids. I wanted to help keep them safe. I guess some kids needed to be saved from themselves also. She was pretty too looked like something from a magazine how could something so pretty do something so evil and nasty. I mean she is a victim of this herself. Her father took something from her at a young age and continues to do so to this day, daily. Her only escape is to get out of here through a school scholarship grant or something. But instead she has accepted it and she passes it along. What she is doing is just breeding some future pedophiles and molesters or giving someone some major trust issues either way the shit that she know is dead ass wrong and has major effects to one's life has to stop. Her being a child puts me in a funny place but the shit that she does puts me in a heated place I mean I'm red hot and sad at the same time. It's some fucked up shit I can't save her she already fully fucked up but I can and will try to save the kids she fuckin with.

I picked up the envelope that said royalty and there was a key and number on it, I knew damn well what the key was to and couldn't wait to skip my happy ass over there to get it. I was blown as hell and geeked all at the same time. I aint never in my 14 years of living held twenty five hundred dollars in my hands able to do whatever I wanted with it and after it's done I get another twenty five hundred. I had to hurry and put this bitch out her misery as Unk would probably say. I started my research that day I told my dad I was going to the pool and to my surprise I didn't even have to get out of taking lil man with me, so I knew today was about to be a good ass day.

I caught the bus to Brandon Towne Center so I could meet up with Von he said he would let me use Unk car to ride to Davis Island he aint want me on the bus or nothing, he had secretly been teaching me how drive. When I seen his ass sitting in front of the car just standing there he looked so good not like a teenage boy but a grown ass man. Made me feel more like a woman who's man was checking for her, yeah we wasn't together but we had dibs on each other.

He greeted me with a hug that lingered longer than usual and a kiss to the fore head. "Call me as soon as you getting ready to leave the store so I can be here. Be careful love." he opened my door shut it and walked off. He was so damned sexy.

When I got to Jet Ski and Thangs by Ben T Davis Island it was crowded that day. On the inside it was a line about three people. I seen a middle age white man, a teenage white male, a college looking white girl moving about the store doing different things I didn't see Kym though and today was Thursday, maybe she was on a break or what if she didn't even work here anymore she is a teenager some of us can't keep a job but I'm a keep mine so this bitch need show her mug. Rite when I was about to be called next in line I seen her standing right outside the window the wind was blowing her long hair it had to reach her ass. She was sporting in what looked like scuba gear it was a shorts set thing she had papers in her hands and she was laughing and talking to an older guy I would've guessed she was instructor or instructors assistant.

"NEXT!!" I heard loud enough to knock me out my thoughts and I seen the college girl with an agitated look on her face. I apologized and let the next person go ahead of me while I watched Kym to figure out my next move. She was really pretty, the type that niggas would be chasing every day for the thrill knowing damn well they wouldn't have had a chance. I could understand a man not being able to resist her but her father though he should have been the one on my list. Maybe I'll just knock him off him for a bonus I mean he the reason I'm killing this beauty. Hmm who knows? I was up at the desk again the Mr. Rogers look alike had finally backed off Kym so now I was on my way to introduce myself. I had to get to her before she walked inside I aint want none of these folks in my business they already gone member me from that lil blackout in line. I hurried out the door.

"Hey girl" I said stopping in front of Kym "Girl you look like you can help me your more my type." I said touching her waist for a brief second. "I mean my type like you can help me better than white whiter and whiten" I said laughing and nodding my head inside. She loosens up and smiled "Well yes ma'am sweetie what can I do to...do for you?"

"You do lessons of scuba diving?"

"Well we do but I don't work on the days that they do the private lessons I work during the open to public classes only."

"Damn" I said stumping my feet.

"What, what's wrong?" She said startled "We still have an hour class left today you can come in I'm there." I looked around then stepped real close to her

"I don't like a lot of people I get uncomfortable can't get the full effect of shit because I gotta watch folk, people crazy and sometimes you just have to sit back to watch, and I like to sit in back and watch everyone. So I know I would not learn shit...got some deep trust issues. If it's just me and you, one on one, I can concentrate a lot better." I said with a smile "Come on, please. Pay is not an issue. I'm spoiled so don't ruin my day plus my Birthday was yesterday!" She was about to say something but I said "Just say yes you have to, we part of the pretty girl club we got to help each other out, we'll have fun." I said looking her up and down. She liked that.

"OK. Look well meet right at that boat docking place on Courtney Blvd. across the street it's a little beach rite before Clearwater rite up over the bridge. Sunday round two O'clock."

"Thank you thank you." I said jumping and clapping.

"It's cool bring two hundred and fifty dollars." Damn two fifty I thought yeah dis bitch need to die. She gave me her cell number which I knew I wasn't finna ever use I confirmed date and time we said our goodbyes then went our separate ways.

Soon as I stepped out the door I called Von to let him know I was on my way back. I sat in the car before I pulled off just thinking my life changed so much in the last seventy two hours. I made amends with my mother. I was now a hired contractor and my first target, a child. I never would have thought I take a child out as a molester a person doing wrong to children I mean I know it happens but I just never thought it would be my reality. On the way to Javon so much was going through my head I don't even remember the drive back to the mall to be honest. When I see Javon's face every little thing every thought any problem was non-existent. He made me happy he filled me up just by being near. I pulled into the spot Von opened my door grabbed my hand and helped me out when I stood directly in front of him he kissed me, just a soft kiss on my lips he did it again then again on each side of my neck.

"You are beautiful what you stand for is beautiful and our empire is going to be beautiful." He said sealing with another kiss, that even though it wasn't tongue involved just the way his lips held mine and didn't want to let go for a couple of seconds it was soft it was wet it was sweet. Von dropped me off at home told me I can use the car Sunday meet him at the same place. He winked and we parted ways.

Sunday was here I was anxious scared relieved all at once talk about anxiety attacks when I pulled into the man made beach there were a few people scattered around sunbathing mostly playing wit they dogs I picked a nice secluded spot on the end under a tree that sun do me good but that shade do me better. I saw Kym over in the water just walking her feet through the water. It was a sad beautiful vision she had to go and today was her Judgment Day.

Walking in the house later that night I felt guilty then a mug. I just knew my dad was gone call me out smell death on me or something, but it was all good. "Oh you becoming a beach bum, working out all the time, you think you grown cause you in high school huh?" I just laughed.

"You said it so it must be true." I and ran up the stairs stripped myself of every little piece of gear I wore today, the clothes I had on when I first went to the scuba shop, and the paper she put her number on all in a paper bag. I would go to Unk and burn all this shit in his back yard the gun was mine. Unk sent me a gun today via Von when he gave me the car, said I was too good to have a lil bitty 22 I needed power. I jumped in the shower and felt good like my cherry was just popped. I felt like I grew up, no more lil sally walker, jump rope, four square, hop scotch, freeze tag, nigga knockin, my child hood was over I was onto adult games now and I had no problem with it because I was now also getting adult money. I couldn't wait to see Von tomorrow so I could tell him every little detail I didn't tell him tonight because I wanted to be able to take my time and act out the scene.

I didn't get a chance to see Von that next day at school. So I was waiting all day to jet off toward Unk crib once that bell struck 2:45 I was outie soon as I got to Unk's house I went straight to back to get that shit up off me threw the paper bag in the trash can and lite the bitch up.

Unk ass snuck up behind me talking bout "Where your boyfriend?" I played his game.

"I don't know he aint here? I have been checking for that boy all day."

We looked at each other shrugged and looked back at the fire he moved some shit around to calm it a little bit.

"So how was it Pretty?" ugh I hated that name. I looked at him and smiled and answered.

"To damn easy, next time I hope they have a challenge." I laughed. He laughed a little too.

"Yeah I picked the right one."

While we were talking Finger one of Unk's right hand men called Unk told him to come here they whispered some shit looking over my way occasionally then Unk told me to watch the fire till it go out then take my ass home just like that. I did what I was told I was waiting on Von anyway but Von aint never show up so I took my ass home he had betta not be anywhere flirting. Me and Von were walking down the beach at Clearwater it was empty out tonight seem like we were the only two out I was rocking this fly ass black and gold baby phat bikini with some Levi jeans I cut up and Von was looking hella good in his Levi jeans and high tops and his crisp white v neck and that Rolex was shining under the moonlight shine.

I was finally telling him about my first hit how I had to flirt with her ass we went got some food after my two hour, two hundred fifty dollar beginner learn the basics class. I should have been a pro for that amount. Kym ordered some pizza and wings she popped her tits up and got us some beers from a horny little clerk. I sat in her car ducked behind her tent while she got everything. We ate a little drank a little talked a minute then she tried to push up on me like rub me a little tryna inter lock legs, so I asked her lets go out in the water for a little while then later we would slide to my house since my folks would be gone for the night and if she wasn't OK with that I told her I knew how to get us a room. Once out there under water I pulled the trigger shot her in her stomach chest and neck, and in that order. While she was sinking deeper each time I got a round off. I thought three would be a charm.

Walking back to Unk car all I seen were her eyes they looked surprised turning into sadness which turned into relief she took a deep breath shut her eyes then said "geulaeseoineun jonglyo bangbeob-ida" that phrase word played over in my head the whole time I sat and watched from the distance. I sat for about thirty forty five minutes until I felt the coast was clear and decided to leave.

I was excited because I was telling a story I needed Von to get it, telling him how I wasn't scared at all it just came naturally. I loved the fact being that I could tell Von anything I wouldn't be one of those people that had a job and had to keep it secret because they don't want that person to judge them or be scarred of them or have their life in danger the fact that he hooked me up with this shows he cares and trust me so I owe my love to him because of him I will be Rich and get the revenge I sought on my offenders. "I wish Jen was here." I said.

"Me too."

"Do you think if Jen was here you would of still hooked me up with Unk or even be here right now? I mean are you close to me because she's gone, or because you want to be?"

He stopped in his tracks while squeezing my hand then faced me to him. Looked me dead in the eyes before speaking

"Girl I love you and whether Jen stayed or not you would be with me here tonight." He reached around my waist and pulled me into him and gave me my very first kiss a passionate kiss. I was melting in his arms I think I even kicked my foot back like they did in those old movies.

"Mina!" I heard but didn't want this moment to end it got louder it sounded like my dad. "Damina!" A hand grabbed my shoulder.

"What!?!"

My father jumped back "I'm sorry Mimi, I aint mean to wake you but Unk just called me and Javon was found murdered tonight right over by Jen's old house." *Wake me? Wait what Von murdered?* I tuned back in to my father. "He went through some type of struggle and been stabbed twice once in the chest and the other in his back."

My head began spinning and palms got sweaty. "Von was murdered?" I blacked out and didn't hear anything else all I could think of was my man was gone and I now had vengeance number 3 on my list the only problem was I didn't know who it was I was looking for but I promise I would find out I know he aint do nothing to anybody so whoever did it did it out of pure hatred. Pops said something to me hugged me then walked out my room. I didn't cry I didn't scream I just lay there I didn't have a plan just yet but I would make one. Preparation meets opportunity a wise man once told me.

Netta B.

# Chapter Nine

July 2012

Look at this lame ass nigga here. He sooo happy to be getting with me jumping, skipping, doing the hula-hoop and shit. You aint even got to wonder who he with or what he finna do, you see it all in his eyes and happy body tone and shit. All this from a nigga who getting money like they say he do it should be no problem getting pussy but then again that simple ass game he tried to throw my way I take that back. Shit I guess every bitch on the block aint that smart it's a lot of green ass niggas and thirsty bitches around too, and that's what his ass needs a bitch he can mold. I wish I could put this L 7 on to game oh well sucks for him. Makes me wonder why the fuck my momma would insult my daddy with this piece of shit nigga. He fucked me over at the age of eleven twelve however old I was and now he fucking with folk's money, look at him he act like the receptionist just gave his ass a million bucks. It's just a room key lame!

Nigga don't even know he walking into his own death trap. I'm his worst kind of enemy a bitch with a vengeance on his ass. He part to blame introducing me to a "real" fuck nigga, the reason for becoming what I am today, it's get back season. Pablo Javon's older half-brother, a brother they found out two years after Von's death. He was deep in the dope game and stumbled up on this nigga here by pure luck. Look at his goofy ass, fucking bum! OK get back into mode Mina. *I want him. I want him! Go!* I thought finding the biggest sexiest smile I could muster up.

"OK baby, I got the keys, herb and yak in back! So let's go to the room so we can rat-ta-tat-tat! I'm-a needa bout a ten hours if you cool with dat."

Oh my gawd! Somebody kill me now L 7 done turned into MC Wacker Lame. I thought "Damn boo I see you got a little rhyme on you love. Let me find out you tryna cross over to the rap game. Matter of fact let me wipe you down lil Boosie." *Or should I say lil dookie cause he gone shit his self-tonight.*

"Hell yea I got rhyme and in a minute you gone feel my rhythm while I'm wiping that ass down. It's a savage life baby."

We both started cracking up when really I was screaming on the inside. If this nigga was Boosie I was Lauren Hill cause he was killing me softly with his words. I looked out the window mainly to roll my eyes.

"Aye so Rey you think my car gone be safe over there at the bar?"

"Yea it should be OK, but we can go back after a while and go get it and bring it back over here so you don't worry about it through the night."

"I don't mind getting my freak on in this lil rinky dink spot cause we can stand up and get to the business but I will not and I repeat will not be sleeping here"

"Yea OK that's what you say now but don't go tryna change your tune later on doe when you find out yam boy doing that!"

He pulled up in front of the room and I was glad I could still see my car. It wasn't really anybody here maybe because it's a weekday or this spot is not the business I really don't know and don't give a damn the quieter the better, less people I have to worry about. Before he even put the car in park he jumps out and bout skips his lil happy butt over to open my door and gets his lil party starters from the back seat. When we get in the room it has the usual bathroom, bed, table, chairs, chained down TV and hot ass room.

"Please turn that air on its hot as hell in this bitch." I complained. I really just didn't want to touch the buttons. I pulled the sheets back cause that was the only place I was sitting mainly because that was probably the only clean thing in here the sheets maybe the table but I doubt that. I grabbed the remote and started flipping channels while Mr. Double L 7 flipped through the radio I guess looking for something to set the mood the appearance alone was killing it then he finally found something which I'm assuming it was 1150 it was Stephanie Milles.

"Oh yea that's what I'm talking bout." he started doing a lil dance with himself first he actually looked sexy to me so I smiled and stared dancing a little "Yea!" he said "Now come over here with your pretty lil self and give me a grown folks dance."

"Oww taking charge. I like that, a real man not a little boy."

"Oh you like that well just wait for the demands and request I got for you later." The thought of him touching me made me sick I wanted to kill his ass now but I'll have a little fun let him be happy before his last breath. In all reality I was so elated to be here with Corey my first offender the nigga that turned my mother against me. His ass was so horny he couldn't even see the death in my eyes, didn't even, haven't even really looked at me. I know I got a wig and shit on but for nigga who was so in love with my mother he can't even see her in me? Now that I was twenty years old I looked like a spitting image of my mother just a little slimmer had her butt. Telling me his name Rey nigga anybody can put together Rey short for Corey and then his dumb ass in Florida not China somewhere you still in the states, but I smiled and stroked his ego I mean I would be the last to do it.

"Oh, demands and request? Slow your roll lil daddy, I mean big daddy we got all night." He started reaching for me. "Chill OK Rey you not allowed to touch the dancers at the strip club so no touching me keep your hands to yourself for now and do me a favor and close your eyes."

I closed my eyes also and wonder why continue to play with him just get to the business but the drink was good the herb was pure and my body was swaying. Inhaling every puff off this medical Cali bud I was feeling good Raheem Devaughn was playing in the back ground and L 7 was looking better every min. I continued to dance for him for one reason it had been a while since I really let my hair down and dance, my love life was down the drain and my sex life right with it except for my occasional Atlanta visits but I was getting bored and restless. I was happy he was in my city doing business. I let him touch me for a while it felt good he grabbed at my waist then the small of my back and slapped my ass at the right angle damn I was getting bothered. I'm glad I could go home after this I had a special friend at the house waiting for me. So what it ran on batteries and didn't hold me, it got the job done that some niggas just couldn't get right. I smiled at the thought while turning to face him giving him a little titty action. "You like that daddy?" I said putting his face in my titties.

"Damn you smell good but I wonder how that pussy smell and taste"

"I am what I eat and I eat good."

"I believe it cause you look good."

I grabbed his hands and placed them on the arm rest

"Hold on to yo seat cause I got something else for you baby."

"I see a better place to hold on to." he said while placing one hand between his legs moaning. He tempted me cause I seen the imprint of his dick and it made me want to let him breathe a little longer but fuck that dis nigga wasn't no good his meter was damn near expired. I walked around him to the back bent down to his ear.

"There you go taking charge again; I guess you are a boss."

"Hell yea I'm a boss a fucking violator." That shit snapped me out my character I was playing he just made me mad as hell it was time.

"You a violator huh?"

"Hell yea over any and everything, shit don't have a chance if I want it or if it's in my way."

"Oh, you are doing it like that huh?"

"Ain't that why you here? Shit, real recognize real."

"It's true boo!" I said giving him a neck massage.

"And when I seen you I seen a real flaw nigga!" By time flaw made it out my mouth I had his thirty seven thousand dollar chain tight in my grip and chocking his ass with it. "That's why my daddy the one you said don't give a fuck about me, he thousands of miles away, came to the "D" and whopped yo goofy ass. A "real" real nigga can't let you fake ass niggas think yawl can't be touched." He was going a lil buck in the chair swing in trying reach for hair and eyeballs calling me bitches and hoes that made me mad low key, I hate being called out my name.

He was my first real piece of vengeance he was the nigga to start this shit from my hate to my drive. I couldn't let people like him live I was one of the stronger ones it's some out there that's not so strong they can't tell, they can't leave; some can't even muster the strength to live. I'm not God and I damn sure aint the devil, but I can decide the fate for these dumb selfish ass fuckahs.

I drought my knee up to the side of his face stuck him good in the temple then banged his head on the single table in room that was in front of him but towards the side hoping I would bust his nose. He stopped all the squirming reaching for his nose I use this time to take my red bottoms to his nuts stuck him two more times in the nose with my knee then punched his ass in the dick this time. Poor lil baby was bout crying now saying he was sorry.

"I was young and stupid and never did no shit like that again. Yo pops taught me my lesson then his boys fucked me up some more later on that day. I'm sorry for what I did; it's no reason for you to be tryna kill me my baby."

I for one knew it was a lie cause in his file it said he was fucking with his niece, his blood sisters own child for the last three years now. I was tired and ready to take his ass out his misery. I bent to his ear. "I'm sorry too. Sorry you got the wrong young bitch to take for a dumb hoe." I tighten my grip on that chain and snapped mister stupid neck all with his own chain. It really don't make any since how easy that shit was niggas stupid and this shit between my legs will always be a man's downfall and some bitches too. But they say it's a man's world that shit just as crazy as it is stupid to me.

PRETTY: Her Introduction

# Chapter Ten

BOOM BOOM!! it's the police open the door or we will break it down BOOM BOOM! I jumped up heart beating fast as hell as I looked around wide eyed wondering what was going on BOOM BOOM!!

"Damina get ya ass up" it was my dad and it was only a dream the police was not out to get me I stretched then reach for my radio to turn it on, a sign I use to tell me pops I'm up. "Bout time, get yo ass up! Damn only hoes and lazy mutha fuckas with no goals sleep past noon."

"You would know. You know enough hoes." I said under my breath

Since that was my cue to get the hell up and out of here I went straight for the shower. I listened to my dad talk to my brother as he walked off. "Lazy ass girl I done spoiled her rotten, and you aren't too far off big head!"

Just as I stepped out the shower and wrapped myself in the towel my home girl Crystal called me she be having radar.

"Hey girl" I answered

"What you got going on?"

"I'm up if that's what you mean. What we getting into today?"

"I don't know I really don't feel like going to the park just come over here and well order something or ask Jah to bring us something from the park she went out there earlier wit one of her dudes."

"Alright let me throw something on I'll be over there in a lil bit."

"OK girl"

"Oh Chrys you talk to Lana?"

"Girl you know I aint seen no damn Lana. I don't know where her ass is. That's yawl crazy ass friend."

"Whatever girl you silly, Ima tell her you said that when I see her again too."

"Bet. I aint scared of her or yo crazy ass." We both burst out into laughter.

"OK girl I see you in a bit and call Lana for me real quick." my call waiting beeped. I hung up "Hey hoe" I said it was Jah she must of felt us talking about her. She was a little angry bird low-key.

"What's up? Yall coming to the park or what? It's kind of thick out today too. It's just too damn hot is all."

"Naw we gone stay in so do your rounds and bring ya ass on with some food when you leave"

"OK boo, I'm finna leave in a little bit… wait hold on what you mean my rounds you think you know me so well little girl."

"Whateva chick just meet us ova there soon."

"Alright bye."

Them my girls Crystal, Khadijah, and Alana were my homies like for real. I don't know why we became so close but we did. We all met at the same time out at Club Underground one night. Trina came into town to perform I had to go cause I love her ass she spoke her mind really saying what every bitch feel, fill me up in the bank first number two being sexually. It's what these niggas was made for to take care of us duh but niggas wanna play with you before they provide for you. Anyway we all ended up sitting at the same table in VIP we all came alone and in between the drinks and finding out everybody bought they own weed too.

We clicked quick, talking reciting lyrics and dancing

like we been down for yrs. At our table all you seen was Louboutin and Gucci shoes and bags, and Badd ass sexy ass bitches, the center of attention to the ones who couldn't see the stage. When the bar was bout over and up an old crusty ass Dominican girl came and shoulder bumped me I sized her up but chummed her monkey looking ass off. Guess she didn't like the no reaction I gave her so she came back and stood right in front of me.

"Do I know you?"

All the girls got quiet and just stood and watched to see what I was gone say. I looked her ass up and down

"Do we even look like we know the same people let alone each other?" I replied turning from her to finish my goodbyes. She grabbed my shoulder and before I knew it I grabbed the first bottle I seen and slung it cross that bitches head she fell out and three other bitches came running towards me and them three bitches by me grabbed one of each. After we drug those bitches around a bit we left went to waffle house where I paid them back with breakfast, we exchanged numbers and parted ways and we been cliqued up ever since.

Crystal or Chrys as I like to call her, she a white girl older than us she was twenty-five real thick with the ass and hips lacking up top though real pretty face not rough and old looking like most white people she look like she gone age gracefully one of the few white people to do it. She still looked like she could be in high school, and most white high school students don't even look like they posed to be there. I guess she felt like a mother to us cause she was five years our senior.

Khadijah I called her Jah, she was cool. She was my age well bout a year older twenty one mixed girl she was black and Korean real pretty girl and real mean too, slim and tall what niggas would call exotic or foreign been through a lot in her life both parents living got two older brothers and a baby sister but she live like they not, like she really out here alone a real fuck what you think type of girl I guess a hustler at heart cut throat slash man eater. Alana doe she was different she was like my ace for real last of the dying breed. She was the scholar looking to change the world type shit a nerd but a socialite she knew everybody and everything a humble type. she was black I mean blue black but so pretty a natural beauty thick perfect eyebrows, straight teeth, one perfectly centered deep dimple on each cheek with cat eyes that went from gray to hazel crazy exchange but it fit in her favor. Lana was twenty like me both Leo's.

We were girls a clique if you will of all shades beautiful uniquely package, bad to the bone and paid. That's the way I liked my circle a few fine females who were their own person, motivated, with standards and goals. Meaning they own fucking life to live and aint worried about mine. Nobody had kids and we weren't nowhere near broke bitches couldn't even see em. Everybody was getting theirs so no jealousy within the clique, and that's the way I like it drama free. We did our own thang mixed with our own dirt when we were apart and on the same thing when we were together.

We was homies have been for the last four years. I was a killer, Chrys has killed, somebody was gone kill Khadijah ass, and Lana was gone be the help from a high place. We were different in many ways but also just the same. I threw on some lounge clothes threw my hair in a ponytail and headed down stairs.

I was feeling anxious on the way down stairs like I needed to hurry up and get out this house my chest was hurting and breathing speed up. This would sometimes happen to me before a kill. I stopped for a minute counted to ten while breathing through my nose. It relaxed me fast and easy. At the bottom and the stairs found the usual scenario my brother sitting in the middle of the couch stunk on the Xbox. I can't be mad cause any other day I would be tryna beat him on some Wii game.

"What's up big head?"

"Be quite!"

"Whateva big head."

I made my way into the kitchen and found the best man in the world with the worst attitude in the world.

"Morning dad!"

"Morning!?"

"What time you on west coast?"

"Sorry bout that I was up there Knocked out too." I said with a lil giggle. He was slightly irritated. I got serious, something was wrong. "I was out a lil later then I originally thought I was finishing up some old business." I glanced at the clock an hour had already passed since I spoke with Jah nem so I was about to cut this short by disappearing. "Look dad I'm bout to head to Chrys house. I'll be back round seven, eight tonight."

"Aye real quick before you leave." there go that pain creeping in again, I got back comfortable on my stool and embraced myself for the wrath. "Look, Damina you got to get a job your well over the age to start working or something. I'm tired of looking at you. How you get money never mind shit you got to many talents you cut my hair to a T can cook your ass off and graduated an honor student. What do you want out of life? What are your goals, when does your life really start? Tell me what you wanna do; I'll put you through school tomorrow. You got till the end of the week to figure out what you wanna do or you going to have to go binge off your mom and help enrich her business so you can do what you want to do, or do what she's been building for you!" *Building for me? I never said I wanted to move back the "D" or run a beauty salon* I thought.

I remember the days leading up to the shop unveil though my dad got her good. Mom's was so happy when he unveiled the salon a gift she never expected. One day I had to be five or six because I believe I was in the first grade. Dad had a big surprise for my mom I remember him teasing her "I got something for you this is going to make you love me even more than you do now." I sat there thinking is that even possible I knew she was crazy about him "...the best surprise I have done this far!" he continued. I think my mom was getting a little irritated and antsy because she jumped up and sat on his lap smiled, batted her eyes then told him more so than asking "If I find it you gotta get me something else to top what I find."

"OK, deal. Go ahead and tear this house up cause you aint gone find it but hey it'll be your mess to clean up" he said laughing

She checked every hiding place she knew of in the house but just couldn't find it. I think she went to sleep mad because of the mess she made without having nothing to show for it, also she knew she would get nothing extra. When she tucked me in she said "That little sneaky man, the gift probably aint even at the house it's probably in the car or just a trip or something." she said kissing me on the forehead. "Silly me" then she got up walking towards the door and turned and said "Don't ever rush, or ask a man anything twice, whatever he wants to do he will do, and if you have a real man like daddy whatever comes out his mouth is golden nothing but the truth. But if his word can't be trusted please leave him just as fast as the lie came running out! He'll respect you more. Good night Ladybug."

The next day while watching TV dad came in the house "Where are my two beautiful ladies?" I looked up and smiled and mom peeked around the kitchen door.

"I'm rite here daddy'o!" she said laughing.

"Since you couldn't find your gift last night and got the house looking so good early this mornin lets go for a ride do whatever mommy wants to do does that sounds like a plan mom and Mimi?"

"Yes! Say yes momma!" I begged I just wanted to get out of the house

"Okay I guess, I was about to start cooking but I guess we could go pick something up I don't mind the break."

"Yes, hunny we can do whatever you like it's all about you" my daddy said rite before flashing his picture perfect smile which my mom loved cause whenever he flashed it she couldn't help but cheese with him.

It was pretty chilly this day out in HP we went for a ride down Woodward Ave. toward downtown Detroit I seen the usual depressing stuff I usually seen on the streets. Couple bums or J's, trash, empty parking lots, gray skies, just so cold and bold out in these streets. Out of nowhere my mom burst out "Bae what is that?"

"What you talking bout?" my dad said sounding slightly irritated.

"Look, in that Plaza. It's a new salon and it's got my middle name in it. Must be a sign." she said touching her hair. "Heavens Hands…I like that name lets go over there real quick." she said sounding as happy as a kid in a candy store.

"The hair salon that's gone take all day" my dad complained.

"You said it was my day big daddy." mom said like

she was finna sock him in the mouth if he denied her. Dad just laughed while turning around and drove the car toward this new spot Heavens Hands. My mom jumped out and practically ran to the door with dad and I a couple steps behind her. "Damn Cal it's closed, it don't even look like its open yet anyway. It look to empty in there look in, it's spacious though what this building use to be?" she said not really asking anybody anything. I just stood behind watching them I was happy it wasn't open anyway I aint want to sit in the shop all day anyway. While mom was all in the window talking bout what she would do to this and that like somebody cared. Dad was walking into the door.

"Look ma." I said pointing at dad.

"Cal wait! What you...they left the door open? Oh they done lost they mind do they know people out here hungry and desperate all this shit could be gone in five minutes or less."

"Well the owners here, and we aint no punks. I wish a nigga would!" he said smiling holding up keys.

"Oh no you didn't, is this, oh my gawd this for me?!? You think you so slick thank you Cal I love it." she said jumpin up and down all happy and shit it's been a min since I seen her like this she was really happy.

"It's all good baby you know whatever you want and need I got you. And even though you aint find this in the house you still found it. So, what do you want? Anything bigger than this million dollar money maker right here? I got you baby we bout to take over the hair capital."

"Usually I would want something else but I got everything I need as of right now a family and my business. I love you Calvin you are truly a blessing. I will always be at your debt."

"No, I'm in your debt for showing me love and

giving me loyalty. I'll give you what you need just stay by my side."

Heavens Hands was open by time summer came I remember because when school ended I started having my days at the salon with my mom. It was slightly slow at first which my mom was fine with because even though this was her shop she didn't have her cosmetology license yet and she was working on it and she didn't want her employees to have more clientele then her. She hired two barbers, two manicurists, a massage therapist, and a tattoo artist she was saving all the hair styling for herself. She would have no competition in her shop she would say. "This my shit and be damned if I be sitting down watching hoes do hair while I'm offering bitches refreshments and shit like I'm a shampoo girl." throwing her neck and rolling her eyes. "Heavens Hands, Heavens Plan" that's what became her new motto. I loved my momma but couldn't stand her at the same time.

# PRETTY: Her Introduction

# Chapter Eleven

I dropped down on my elbows on the counter in front of me he just knocked me down a couple of feet wasn't expecting that it's not like I can't afford to live on my own I just don't want to. I never ask him for money and I'm rarely here, and I pay him a fee of one hundred fifty dollars a month not that he ever asked.

"Are you kicking me out?"

"That's up to you." He started walking towards me "It's always been up to you, but you're taking a little too long so I'm helping you out pushing you a little, you got your little brother. I need good examples round here. I need him to know a good woman, one with work ethic, motivated." he kissed me on the forehead then went back to making lunch or putting it up whatever he was doing.

I sat and watched him for a little bit then went and sat on the couch where my brother was. My dad was a good man, a realist, very hard worker. He'd always say "I'm the money man and money is the plan." while putting money into one of his three hiding places he had stashed in the house in the "D" one he say was ours as a family, one for mommy, and one for me. Only me and daddy knew about the stashes he said mommy would shop all our money away. When daddy came to get me I grabbed our money and left only half of ma's stash, it seemed fair. Another reason why I say he was a good man he left the money when he could have easily taken it I mean she didn't know about it. When Calvin Jr. came into the picture I gave little brus the half of ma's money that I took if daddy took him in with no problem so could I. He didn't like confrontation and loved woman and his kids and I loved him. While watching my brother I wonder would it be better for just the men to be in the house.

I remember when big head came ten years ago I wasn't expecting it and I know dad wasn't expecting some woman at the door like here is your son if you don't believe get a DNA test. You the only nigga I been wit. Yea I was cheating on my man, with you but he is white so this aint his. They stared at each other for while it seemed like slow motion. That shit blows me every time I think about it. I love him she started again. I told him I would give my baby up for adoption but I'm not doing that not when I know the daddy is perfectly fit. Please just take care of him for me, his name is Calvin Larry Rose, named after you. He fresh out the box! My man does not want to look at another man's child. I love you but I'm in love with him. She handed over the delivery. He waiting on me, I gotta go! Is basically how that went when I think about it.

That is how she presented lil man. Both of us there with our mouths wide open shocked like a mutha fucka. All I could think about is if this bitch lying I'm a find her myself and beat her ass. I already wanted to sock her in the mouth for taking my case of the only child from me. But I grew to love him he was me. I mushed my brother then whispered big head he tried to shove me he missed I did it again this time getting in his view.

"DAD!!"He bout lost his damn mind

"Dad I'm about to go, I'll let you know by Friday. I said while making my way back to the kitchen to grab my purse off the counter.

"Love you, be good Damina. And just in case you

don't find your way home tonight call me so I know what's going on. You know how you do."

"I won't be gone long dad" I went to hug my brother irritate him a little bit more.

"Get off me I'm tryna beat a high score."

"Love you too big head." I said walking out the door.

"You got your memory cap on?" That meant pay attention to what I'm going to tell you. so I put my Coney dog and fries down, sat up straight and tried to soak in every word he was about to lay on me. "Remember this if you don't remember nothing else I tell you." he always said that before everything he told me but I'd remember it all. His words where the truth in my eyes.

"OK" I said

"You are beautiful"

"Thank you dad, people say..." I started but he cut me off quick

"Listen Damina." he said my whole name so if I was about to play and get silly that quickly changed. He started over. "You are beautiful, you are intelligent, you are a lady, you deserve the best, you will strive for the best excelling in all that you do because you only follow your heart, trust no one but yourself, preparation meets opportunity, and be the best you can be. Remember those eight things and you will be OK. Okay?"

"Yes sir." Those were easy things to remember I thought he was gone give me a challenge I thought.

"I'm moving from Ferris"

"Don't move further please

"I sorry but I have to" I knew where but I was hoping I was wrong he was talking about to Florida.

"Do you have to move to Florida now can't you wait a while?" he looked shocked when I said it like how she found out who told her but relieved also like yea this my daughter.

"Yes, I have too and I want you to visit every summer it's all kind of water parks out there beaches did you know Disney world was there we will have so much to do once I get settled."

"Ok" I really just wanted to scream, fuss, and kick throw a big fit but I sucked it up and went back in on my Coney dog and chili fries. I knew this day was coming I just wasn't ready.

"You still got on your memory cap?" he asked. I wanted to say fucked yo memory cap nigga take that shit with you instead I just shook my head yes. He said "Look at me Damina" this full name shit was getting on my nerves as well. "I love you, you are my one and only true love whatever you need I will make sure you have it. If anybody is messing with you, you let me know and I will handle it. Just because I'm moving does not mean I don't care. Your all I care about, you are my heart, whatever you need I'm there for you. Do you understand?"

"Yes sir."

Leaving my daddy that night was hard I went home took a bath and went straight for bed. Mom asked if I was going to stay up and watch TGIF with her but I wasn't up for it. I didn't feel like laughing I just wanted to lay down and think. In the middle of the night I guess my mom heard me sniffling she came in and asked me what's wrong. I told her must of been the food I ate when I was with daddy. She tried to rub my back for me I asked her to stop and leave me alone. I mean she was the reason my heart was broken. She did what I asked and left me alone. I cried all night until I fell asleep.

The next day it was a Saturday because I remember singing the Washington bill song when dad popped up. We went walking he gave me a piece of paper with two numbers on them that weren't Detroit numbers and a pager number that was a Detroit number and he gave me a pager he didn't give me the number he just said whatever number shows up on here you call it. this so I'm always available you never have to hesitate and that pager is just between me and you I don't think your mom would try and keep us apart but I don't want her to be able to go that route if it does cross her mind.

"This is the preparation like preparation meets opportunity?" I asked

"Oh you keep the memory cap close I see."

"In my back pocket"

"Well this is preparation to keep my lifeline and you are my lifeline don't think I'd function properly without you."

Damn he had me goin all down memory lane today.

# PRETTY: Her Introduction

# Chapter Twelve

My phone started vibrating in my pocket nearly caused me to swerve into incoming traffic. It was Chrys.

"Pulling up right now bout to park, open the door."

"Hey boo!" Chrys greeted me at the door. Chrys was pretty as hell she was white but the way she carried herself her shape style down to her talk made you wonder what nationality she was, what she was really mixed with. She stayed out in Apollo beach somewhere I liked she been through a couple thing's so I can relate to her. Lana was over on the couch going through her phone she flashed a smile and winked at me one of things she started doing a while ago it was her hello and her everything is OK signal.

"You see I found cho girl. happy now and I told her that shit you talking on the phone bout you aint scared and you'll fuck her up" Chrys said laughing Lana chuckled a little and looked at me

"Oh what's that again Mimi?" I started laughing

"Girl I say anything when I first wake up. I'm sorry." we all burst out laughing

"What movie yawl wanna watch?" Chrys asked

"I don't care, let's laugh put on that Paper Soldiers or Killa Season."

"You went back. I aint seen them in a while member All about the Benjamin's or should I say Uptown Saturday Night now those are my joints!" said Lana

"Girl it don't matter you pick Chrys!"

"Uh oh what's the matter" Chrys asked

"Nuthin!"

"Yea rite, yo ass don't have an opinion so it's definitely something going on Mina."

"It really aint that deep, nothing I can't fix. I just gotta make up my mind."

"What? Can't figure out what you're going to wear on your next date or how your next hair-style is going to be? Oh I know, you tryna think of a not so messy murder for next time." I rolled my eyes and even smacked my lips but I had to laugh a little at that.

"Damn I got real problems too I am human..."

"Well tell me all about em... wait lets order some food then well get to the problem solving"

"Oh I already talked to Jah. Girl she called right after I got off the phone with you, she gone bring us some barbecue from the park after she do whateva she doing out in that heat."

"Oh OK ahead of the game like always I see"

"Somebody got to do it!"

"OK so what's the problem miss ahead of the game?"

"I need a job."

"Why? You hood rich you got the type of money people kill for no pun intended." She says no pun intended but there was always a pun.

"My dad gave me an ultimatum."

"Oh OK I can see that happening Mr. Cal don't play he got like 50-11 hustles and on top of that pimpin aint easy." Chrys chimed in.

"Girl!" I busted out laughing "I know rite! I don't want no nine to five slaving for minimum wage and that's all I would get with no prior job experience and I'm straight cause of them licks I been hitting and that's getting old I'll be twenty-one tomorrow nine years of that shit is enough, two years of training and seven years of dealing. I think I should have enough money to find those last two fuck boys then chill"

"I feel you on that Smoking Aces." Lana said laughing.

"Don't you have a bartending license." asked Chrys.

"Yea"

"Well go get a job working four days out the week at a strip club and I'll look around for a more elite establishment for little miss pretty."

Lana looked up like what the fuck yawl hoes talking bout. She sat up straight so I knew she was bout to say some serious shit. "Look Mimi maybe your dad know that you got some other shit going on but him being a man of the G code he don't really ask questions cause you handling your business so well he don't even know what you into. Maybe he saying invest in something start up a little business pay some taxes so nothing can't come back and bite you on the butt. I could be wrong or I could be right. Chrys idea was butta too cause the club it's untraceable for waitress and dancers you can say you made whateva." she said then balled back on the couch and back to her phone.

"Ok, I feel you and it's true. I'll start off light at the club till I know what it is I really want to do what I want to put my money in and to keep pops off my case. Thank you boo's" I said giving hugs. The doorbell and the knocks brought me out my thoughts it had to be Jah.

"OK heifer!" Chrys said opening the door. Yea, it was Jah

"Delivery!" Jah said.

"Come in but you aint getting no tip frowzy ass!" Chrys said. We all had to giggle at that one.

"Whateva" Jah said. Her and Lana did they whole

head nod thing they had a love hate relationship going on.

"Hey killa! She said to me that was her nick name for me.

"Whateva hoe!" And that was mine for her "What could you salvage!" I said smelling spices all up and through the air

"Burgers, ribs, mac and cheese, corn, beans, sausage, and some of them sweet Hawaiian rolls." she said like she hit the lottery

"I love them rolls" said Lana

"Me too" chimed in Jah. Finally a subject they genuinely agree on

"Then I guess we watchin All about the Benjamin's since Jah loves this movie and she came through" Chrys said putting the movie in.

"doo doo doopt doo forty-five forty-seven!" We all happened to say on cue then burst out laughing and began fixing our plates.

Netta B.

# Chapter Thirteen

August 2012

My birthday was finally here, it was Leo season. I would be twenty one at midnight tonight on that good Kush and alcohol feeling nice and turnt. I would be grown and official tonight no more tryna sip a bitch drink I could hold my own,  couldn't go in every club just yet but that was OK because I wasn't the club rat type. Tonight I was going for the make a nigga get whiplash and make the bitches wonder if they really were straight look.

I would be on point tonight I just came back from Atlanta like 3hrs ago. I only went because I had to get my hair done and get it done right so I went to Minglee a girl I met at a salon Glam Bar baby girl slays. Then I had to hit up Philips to get my eyes and brows done and Lenox to hit up Bebe Gucci and Carols Daughter even had some birthday sex up there waiting on me, so thus far it was a good twenty first. Getting back home to Tampa I had to get soaking in my lil hoe bath and take a lite nap, so I'm ready for what the night brings. My girl sweet gloss a make-up artist from the "D" beat my face for me had me looking magazine ready. I'm already a diva but she bring that extra up outta me.

Chrys called me right when I was done, like always must be white people radar. "Girl you ready yet?"

"Almost, let slip on my fit and I'm done."

"OK hurry up we waiting, see you in a min."

Here she go rushing me, they been doing good all day not bothering me. She probably wanted to ask and say more but decided against it when she heard my voice, and that's a good thing. I'm sure she called me earlier and wondered where I was. I didn't take my phone when I went to Atlanta it was sitting right here on the bed. I didn't turn it on till I woke from my nap, I seen all those happy b-day text messages, Twitter, Facebook, and even a S/O on IG I was so tickled and thrilled I haven't checked my voicemail yet but I'm sure my mom left a message on there wishing me an happy birthday she never forgets and always sings too. Her butt can't really sing but she makes me smile I always feel the love.

Anyway doe tonight was my night. I loved this Bebe dress and Louboutin shoes I picked up today and it fit my 5'6 128 pound frame like a glove painted on and the shoes making my legs look extra sexy long, posing in the mirror like I was preparing for Americas Next Top Model the petite cycle. My bedroom phone rang.

"Hello?"

"Mina"

"What up Jah?"

"Your highness, can you hurry the hell up?" she said laughing.

"I'm walking out right now!" I should have known it was one of them just checking to see if I was still at the house or on the way some people think they got all the sense in the world. I grabbed my bag to go with my reds bottoms feeling like Trina *Step Step* I couldn't even front standing there looking in the mirror tonight I looked like I was the founder of MGC. I pulled myself from the mirror and headed towards the door and in comes my pops I aint seen him all day because of my running around.

Tonight he was decked out had on Gucci suit, Gucci shoes and a black Movado sport watch. Came strolling in with some little girl, a new one because I aint never seen her before. She was pretty though kind of basic had a lil guess fit seen those shoes at bakers a lil thin gold chain with a bracelet to match looked 14kt had shaved side with natural little ringlets falling, face plain, lil gloss, and no purse. Cute but looked young but whatever that's they thing.

"Hey baby girl. Happy Birthday!"

"Thanx dad."

"This is my friend Tamera."

"Hi, how you doing? Happy Birthday girl you look good." she said clinching on my daddies arm and smiling

"Thank you" was all I said with a smile then looked at my dad

"That last discussion still stands. You need any money?"

Now I don't why this man would ask me that, he know what I'm a say. Yes, whether I got some or not. I held out my hand and smiled "Always!" he handed me three bills.

"Enjoy yourself and wear your safety belt tonight Mina." then did his usual forehead kiss.

"Yea OK you too dad!" I said with a smile and a gotcha face.

I was on my way to parrrtae and I was so excited. I loved when my birthday came around it wasn't really like I got the best gifts in the world or anything cause I could get whatever I wanted, whenever I wanted. I just liked it because it was my day the one day where I was to be praised as far as I was concerned if not praised at least wished a happy wonderful day cause it was my day. On the way to Chrys house I decided to ride the streets instead of jumping on I-4 I-75 or I-275 I wanted to see what was going on up and through the city tonight. I ended up on Hillsborough stopped at the liquor store off 40th and got some raspberry Ciroc then I had to stop at Hillsborough and 34 at this gas station it was jumping over here cars and bodies everywhere not my type of crowd really but you can't look past all this black beauty I seen some of the sexiest successful men known come from the hood and I seen one looking me dead in my face as I high stepped it into the store I knew he would be in there shortly after me, his body said it all. I went inside to do a fill up on the necessities blunts, gum, cranberry and pineapple juice this way I don't have to make any more stops tonight I'm just riding and getting fucked up. Just as I looked up guess who was in front me?

"Damn that smile sexier than that walk you got." I smiled and said "You sure." as I walked off I went and got the cranberry and orange juice while looking for my favorite stride gum sweet peppermint. I happen to look up when I hear the cashier say "Whud up Tae?" and my eyes lock with Mr. Dark and handsome I smiled and made a face like what you looking at then continued with my search looking for my sweet peppermint stride. Mr. sexy can get it if I meet him out in Hype Park somewhere along Bay Shore or something but he was right here in the hood in the middle of shit and aint no telling what he into. I heard him and the cashier share some words and then finally he left which gave me the go ahead because I was not tryna get up close and personal with anybody today. While in line my phone beeped it was my girl Ade a weird name for a girl I would think this to be a man's name but her parents say royalty is royalty man or woman and that's what Ade means royalty so hey whatever.

"Hey girl, what's up?"

"Happy G day my baby!"

"Thank you Ade. You gone come out with us tonight right?"

"Where yawl going again?"

"We finna go to Channel Side AJA come thru, we got some tables some bottles. I aint with the young shit dumb shit tonight. I know they stay crowded that's why I got three tables just so I can move and don't have to knock a bitch out for being all in my space. I wanna be fucked up and have space to move ya feel me?"

"Girl you know I do."

I paid for my shit and went on bout my business I had a celebration to attend. I was almost inside my car when I heard a voice "Excuse me miss can I talk to you for a minute. I smiled held up a finger Ade text me and let me know what you gone do so I can be looking out for you. I hung up the phone. Put my bags in the car then turned to Mr. Sexy.

"So how can I help you? You lost?"

"May I please have honor of knowing your name, and I don't seem to be lost anymore."

"I'm Damina and I'm glad you found your way."

"I'm Bricks!"

"Huh? *Dis that shit I be talking bout!* No baby your real name?"

"My bad Ms. Officer I'm Devontae. Am I who you looking for, if so you can take me in now!"

"Naw, I'm not gone cuff you just yet." he started to laugh and I did too a little but what I was really thinking, if I see you again you good as mine. "Well it was nice meeting you Devontae." I said beginning to close my car door he was about to say something but I cut him off

"Look I got people waiting on me so I'll catch up

with you later Devontae."

"Well damn, like that?"  How am I posed to get up wit you again?"

"Tampa really not that big Boo, I'll see you again!" I said now beginning to back out my spot, I gave him a little smile though. He was the sexiest little thing I've done seen in a long time round here in Tampa I really might have to give him my number next time I see his fine black ass.

I called Chrys as soon as I pulled up, and they had the nerve to ask me to come in. Ohh no ma'am these hoes rushing me telling me to come on I done rushed but still took my sweet time and these tricks tell me to come in this bitch. I open the door they aint even down stairs to greet me aint no radio on in this bitch and it's looking all sad up in this mutha fucka

"Yall rushing me and you aint even ready. This why I..."

"Happy born day miss pretty!" said Chrys coming up behind me, she handed me a little blue box from one of my favorite stores with everyone close behind her.

"Dayum! Thank you girl this hoe sharp I can rock this tonight. "It was a Tiffany's 1837 WIDE it was like a pink rose gold color. On the top in the open space she engraved "Pretty" in cute little cursive writing. I would have gotten sterling silver and no writing. I never thought to put my name Pretty on anything. So this was cute and personal. I loved it. I gave Chrys a tight ass hug "I wanted one of these rings just aint have the time to go get one made or really know what I wanted it to say but you did that C."

"I guess she done gave you a second gift" Jah sour ass said

"Girl yea! Look aint that joint cute."

"I thought we was only giving one gift." I about snapped on that hoe before Lana chimed in.

"Girl shut up it's her birthday, fuck you mad for?" Chrys jumped back in "Girl don't trip. All I did was buy one of the three tables she got at the club tonight but she could of bought the whole club for the night if she wanted to. I wanted to get something she could remember on her 21st, damn party fuckin pooper."

"Whatever, gone and trick off for her. But she grown now just turned twenty one just in case you forgot spoiled as hell and aint worked a day in her life, least no real job. Where my big ass birthday ring at? You got me a day at the spa."

"And that shit cost more than that ring. Don't front you know that shit was nice, five stars hoe." Chrys spat back.

This bitch was tripping. She was throwing my ass off with this little girl temper tantrum and I wasn't wit it. Tonight was gone be all good, no drama in or out the clique. Oh no ma'am! Right now I'm bout my issue! Talking bout me like I'm not standing right here it was my turn to speak. "I'm sorry but if you stop being so fucking hateful and little practical with your money you could be on my level too having people give just to give and money running over. But you weak as hell and dead ass wrong for that jealous shit WE don't even put up with. So bump what you talking bout. I'm celebrating my birthday you coming or nah?" and that's how I felt.

"Fuck yawl hoes too, let's go!" Jah said she knew what was up.

"Before we leave let's take some shots of this Hennessey white loosen up some of this tension. That's why I only fuck with yawl sometimes. Messy ass hoes" Lana said then she burst out laughing. "Yall hoes done started."

We took our shot, well four to be exact. Rolled bout eight blunts then headed for the door it was after midnight and officially my birthday.

"Dang! Look at that line."

"I know rite I feel for them, we straight doe. Pass the blunt Smokey."

Between that strong ass glass of Ciroc I had at the house, those four shots and that granddaddy we just burnt, I was feeling too fucking good all I wanted to do was vibe I wasn't with the dumb shit tonight. I was looking good feeling good and so were my girls. We threw the keys to valet and let the crowd part for us to come through. Me in my Bebe and red's Lana in her Herve Lerger with red bottoms and Hermes clutch the only one of us to carry a purse in so she was holding everything, Jah in some gear called Kaotic Von with her Giuseppe's and Chrys was rocking a Dereon body suit with pockets and Dereon peep toe booties all I heard in my head was Trina...*and aint nuthin you can do about it killing you hoes!* I was feeling too good and getting into AJA was no problem like I planned on it not to be but it was so crowded and so live we got escorted to our tables they brought our bottles. We ordered some wings. I was chilling in my little spot. Club was live doe.

"Girl it's thick as hell in here and I know you see all the glitter sparkling Mina, I'm sure you'll find one up in here tonight!"

"Yep..." right when I was finna read her ass bout finding me a man. I heard the Dj shout me out then my joint by Jrod came on "it's my dawg birthday, it's my dawg birthday! Jump on the D...." I stood on the chairs and cushions why, I don't know I felt I had to. We was wilding Lana and Jah was fucking shit up with their moves all that left cheek right cheek body movement bringing even more eye movement our way. It was kind of weak in the men department that night and I really don't do dreads even though my first and only love Von had them on his lil slim chocolate frame. Damn I missed him he was more than a secret lover but a friend we had a understanding a bond. In this crowd there was no one I was feeling no one who I could even see as a comparison. It was after one a.m. so it was still cool but bout to get stupid dumb thick real soon. I was vibing in the chair talking to Lana crackin on bitches and niggas then my song came on and I practically broke my neck tryna get to the middle of floor to get my dance on. *Like a crash dummy. Bend it ova, touch ya touch ya toes for me. Shake that....* While I was dancing I felt eyes on me something made me look up and there he was Mr. sexy himself and he was staring hard like he aint had his eye candy in a while so I gave it to him good with a extra helping. I started gyrating to every word popping to every beat and every 808 that dropped I dropped with it. *If you having fun in the club, throw ya pumps up. All my ballers in the building throw ya 1's up. If you aint throwin no money get cha funds up. I asked her....*

I wasn't trying sweat but more like trying to make him sweat it was somebody next to him that was tryna talk to him but when he realized what sexy was looking at I had his attention too. Look like buddy said something about me but sexy cut that shit short I acted like I wasn't pressed I just smiled and continued to dance turn a few bums down on the dance floor but I seen everything, baby and I knew yet again by the end of the night he would be in my VIP section tryna figure me out.

In route to my section I was about to straight stone cold a nigga he act like I just couldn't pass finally the nigga caught the clue and bounced. Somebody else grabbed my hand again causing me to snatch my hand away ready to fight at this point "Excuse me but can you please let my damn han...."

"What's wrong, cat got ya tongue?"

"See I told you Tampa wasn't that big."

"What's good, so now I know it's meant to be!"

"Word?! What a strong analysis."

"Didn't I tell you I was a doc, M.D. feel good?"

"Oh so you think I need treatment?"

"Give me your number and we will fill out an assessment."

"Sexy and clever two points."

"Smart and beautiful ten points."

"I love being in the lead" I said smiling I couldn't help but stare at this man he was truly fine and we bumped into each other twice in one night on two different sides of town. I took this as a sign took his phone and put my home number in it didn't want him to be able to contact me directly whenever he wanted to just yet. I slide him the phone with just my number if he wanted it he'd put my name in it and press save. "Don't take too long, I'd hate to forget you."

"A minute is too long, and I hate being forgotten" he messed around and kissed me on the forehead real quick I couldn't believe he pulled my daddies move on me in the damn club.

"Who was that Mina?" Chrys ass snuck up behind me

"Not sure but I'm a find out soon."

"And make sure you let me know because I never forget a face."

I sure hope this heifer aint tryna tell me she had that dick because I don't share dick and I really want some of his. I got a plan for him that's the only reason he the only mutha fucka I seen in the whole gas station I can't remember another niggas face, let a alone the nigga standing next me So yea he mine, now I wonder how long it's going to take till I get a change and play with him. I couldn't wait. I was really feeling myself rite now I needed some dick. Good thing I got some in the A because I'd really be all up in his shit tonight. I thought as I laughed at myself. Another two bottles were sent our way the waiter tells me it's from the gentlemen over there pointing at Devontae and he has a message he says a min is too long when I looked at Tae he was smiling he winked at me then turns and starts back up with the man next to him

"Aye ladies here are two more rounds to put on ice." I looked at Chrys then added "from mystery man of the hour" It was a good ass night we was live till I dropped everybody ass off at Chrys house. Loved em but I needed my bed, it was a long busy non-stop day, so I took my ass straight home. I had a good morning, evening and night or should I just say I had a good day. Shit I'm twenty-one now the fun begins.

Netta B.

# Chapter Fourteen

Yes!!! It was a dream come true Jackie Long had somehow found me on twitter followed me and DM me for the number said did I want to chill for my birthday. *Umm h ell yea!* We was chillin out in Clearwater beach like either of us needed a tan, but whatever I'll put in my time. I could see he was feeling me as matter fact he was about to go in for the kiss before his fucking iPhone started actin all crazy then my cell phone started ringing I was reaching to get it but I was about to fall off my chair then that's when I woke up it was just a dream and my imaginative ass was lying on the floor from the fall out the bed like always irritated and pissed and not caring who was about to be on my line.

"What!?"

"It's 2pm in the afternoon no wonder why you don't age you sleep all fucking day boo!" It was Chrys all fuckin chipper and shit I guess she aint realize I was real agitated

"Man what do you want?!?"

"Get up lets go to the park they having a block at cypress!"

"Okay that's what's up I'm a call you in an hour and half." I said tryna sound nice but letting her know at the same time get off my phone and don't say shit else. I'm guessin she caught my drift

"Alright, cool" she said before she hung up. I fluffed my pillow covered my head closed my eyes and tried to think of where I left off and then it rang again.

"Hoe I said a hour and half!" I said bout to have convulsions.

"What up Mina?" a familiar voice said but I couldn't put a name to it. "Hello? Damina you there?"

"Yea who is this?" I said not feeling like playing any games

"My bad this Devontae I aint know you was a player like that by the way you was turning them around last night."

"Naw that's not my status." I said realizing it was mister sexy from last night. "I just didn't think you would call so soon."

"I told you couldn't do a minute, let alone the night."

"Well thank you for the champagne my girls loved it."

"Fosho so what you got up for today momma."

"Probably going to the park. What about you?"

"It's still in the wind."

"I can dig it but look I was resting I'm going to call you a lil later."

"Oh you just gone chump me off huh? It's cool I'll be waiting.

*****

All I'm doing is getting a job. This is easy as hell you get all that you want all the time you can get a regular job be straight forward look in the eyes don't bit your tongue just be quick, smile, and kiss ass even the smelliest ones. I said to myself while I gave myself the once over up in the mirror. In the middle of my prep talk I heard what sounded like a thunder rolling but the sky looked clear as day then I heard voices and the noise becoming closer I looked in my arm rest making sure my revolver was still there looking over my shoulder realizing it some chicks laughing and talking probably the next shift of dancers because it was their bags I heard rolling on the cement. I watched the girls laughing and talking they were some pretty ass girls looked like my type of friends pretty face pretty body well put together appearance wise but job wise not my thing. I need to tighten up I was acting like I finna go audition for a strippers position. I got out the car did a look over using the car as a mirror fixing my skirt and making sure the twins up top where siting right and they were sitting lovely OK girls let's get it!

When I went into the club I had to let my eyes adjust I didn't know it would be so dark in here. The first person I seen was a black lady looked like she was bout in her thirties, she was pretty but looked like she had a rough night and didn't want to be here at the time. "Hey. How are you doing this morning?" I said with a smile hoping it would rub off on her but it was true the funky attitude that I was feeling was real and she couldn't be broken. She just looked at me.

"Ten dollars."

"I just came in to speak with your shift manager." she said something and pointed. I wasn't even finna give this rat the joy of getting an attitude. "Thank you girl" and I kept it moving. I didn't have time for the silly games kids played I was twenty one now in the words of Wiz Kalifah I'm on my level and me getting on hers might get her fucked up. I walked in looked around and seen a man sitting at the bar he had a walkie-talkie in his hand so I figured he held some type of position here. Of course I had to do my sexy walk towards him he could probably help me and if he could I'd give him a reason to want to. When I got to him he wasted no time.

"Hey beautiful do you need help?" ready to spit his

tired game.

"Yes, I need...can you please direct me to the shift manager."

"Well you looking right at him." he said looking like he had just won the lottery happy but tryna be cool at the same time turning his whole body towards me "How can I help you?" While he gave me all his attention I smiled hitting a stance then putting my hand out to shake his.

"Hello. Nice to meet you I'm Damina. I am a licensed bartender graduated from ABC Bartending School here in Tampa and I am ready to start using my license. I have no kids or significant other I said slightly leaning into him and smiling I have transportation and can start ASAP tonight if needed. I know I had the job he was so deep in my titties I don't think he noticed that I finished so I cleared my throat "Yep and that's about it so can you use me" he must of like the way that sound because he began to cheese.

"What did you say your name was again beautiful?" he said

"Damina but you can call me Mina for short Handsome" I said smiling in my opinion laying it on thick a little too thick if you ask me

"Sexy with personality equals tips." he said looking me up and down my name is Dave and you can start tonight be here at 8pm.

"OK. Thank you!!!" putting on my "I appreciate it so much face."

"No problem just don't let me down if you work out here there may be other opportunities for you in the near future."

"Thank you Handsome I mean Dave."

"It's all good see you in a little bit Mina."

That shit was too easy if I could lure a nigga to kill him I guess I could get one to give me a job. He talking bout future opportunities yea right I got your number I hope you don't think I'm a be shaking my ass for lil to nuthin five hundred to a thousand a night would have been good if I didn't ever get introduced to it as a child that's one hundred percent less than what I made my first kill. I got a different money lifestyle, that grand here and there don't impress me. Bad enough I'm going to have to sit and watch him exploit those silly ass hoes mixed with a couple smart ones in the mix. Girl at the front probably a dancer too that's why she so mad, shit I don't know and I don't care I thought walking to the whip I could of swore I heard my name being called but the door to the club was closed and I didn't see nobody but a drunk girl between two cars bent ova looking a mess and it aint but eleven seventeen AM. Shit was sad. I continued digging in my Gucci bag for my keys. I thought I heard my name again but I don't know nobody out this way so I knew I was trippin then the shit got closer.

"Mimi, girl I know you heard me callin you!!" It was Jah she was the little drunk thang between the cars, and I smelled trouble. "I could tell by that lil stank walk that was you" see here she go, bout to start. "What's up you gotta kill that nigga Dave next huh, marking ya victim, yea watch him he a slick nigga somebody need to kill his ass." she thought that shit was so funny cause her drunk ass was all on my car laughing and shit like it was so funny and she was so serious too I would a laughed too if it wasn't so fucking hot out here but she was trippin as of a lot lately, so I was about to cut this short.

"If you must know I just got a job up here I start tonight." her mouth dropped all open. "Girl you want a ride home, you look crazy out here."

"Naw I'm good, I'm bout to go back inside. I aint

peg you for stripper the type doe, but you do got the body for it girl you full of surprises. Next you gone be telling me you like girls, these niggas need to watch out for you pretty bitches. Especially you, you fine get money and you'll kill a bitch, you a triple threat." she said like she was really puttin on a public service announcement.

"Whateva hoe let me take your drunk ass back in here." I took her back inside and got her some water from the looks of it they know her and really wasn't study-in her ass when I was walking up to Dave still with Jah in tow and still tryna keep my sexy he looked like he wanted to say hell naw. Don't bring her ass my way but it just couldn't come out.

"Um Dave keep an eye on this one for me baby please."

"I got her love"

"See you later girl." she said leaning one arm on Dave. He looked at her out the corner of his eye like girl get your hands off me now look.

"Tonight Mina and don't be late."

Riding home I felt some type of way Jah ass had been tripping lately throwing shade on my gift, and then all in the streets talking all loud and shit bout what I do on top of being drunk so early in the damn day. I aint like that sloppy shit she was doing. I wish she tell a nigga what the fuck she going through I'm sure one of the three of us can help her ass out. I wasn't bout to dwell on that thought. I pulled up to the house so I could go give pops the news that I was doing something with the talk he gave me. Hope it would be good enough for right now.

"Hey big head, where daddy at?"

"I'm in here Mina. What up!"

"Oh nothing just want to know if you have reconsidered the ultimatum you gave me?" I said as I sat at the island in the kitchen and looked at him his face said it all so I just continued on with my little speech "Well I knew that would be your answer, so I'm happy to say I just came from a job interview and I was hired! Over there at Hush Inc." my pops look up so quick looking confused too kind of hurt then mad.

"I said get a job not a gig you aint gotta go stripping Mina I know it's a job but that aint the one I had in mind for you. That shit don't count I'll send your ass off before I let you stay up in here doing that I kn....."

"Dad I'm not a stripper I'm using my bartending license I'm bartending up there." I had to cut him off real quick because he was about start ranting. His face seem to express a little relief "Chill out you know I don't have enough gulls to be bucked naked on a stage and definitely not one where you and your friends be at." he looked up and laughed.

"Slow ya roll like yawl young-ins say."

"I just wanted to let you know you're stuck with me a lil bit longer. I'm about to rest a little before I gotta be back up there at eight tonight."

"I'm glad you took our talk seriously sleeping beauty next talk gone be about getting you a house spoiled ass lil girl."

Walking up to my room I couldn't help but think and thinking damn my first real job. I aint need this money I can buy that club and build me and my dad each a house. I just aint never have no job I hope I don't have no problems.

Damn, sometimes I wish I could just tell my dad that I'm a killer that I get money too we aint no broke Joe's he can basically have anything he want. Dad I'm a killer been laying em down since I was fourteen at the age of eleven moms boyfriend put me through a little trauma and at the age of twelve, a cracker yo homeboy had told me I was supposed to take a ride to the house with him I trusted him on a count of your name and he tried to take advantage of me from it. I started off getting paid five grand and now I'm getting fifty grand some special ones I hit for hundred thousand g's so for seven years I have been working. Who's to say he won't turn me in? Then I got TBD, FBI, SSI, or some shit on my tail, call a doctor on me or just tell me to stop. I can't stop I got two more people on my own personal list to touch shit he'll never know what I do. I can't take the change I'm sure he thinking something though something like I'm runner mule or something like that I hate to say it but maybe even a escort the way I dip in out two and three days maybe even a week, and I stay in the latest he aint stupid. He just don't want to know what it is he see I'm handling it and bringing no one else in on my business. Really I just learned from the best sometimes you just have to keep some things to yourself the less people know the better and more natural and less guilty they look.

# PRETTY: Her Introduction

# Chapter Fifteen

September 2012

"Girl I miss him."

"Here we go again, every ti...." Aww shit here we go Chrys and Jah ass I thought

"Every time what hoe? So what I can morn, I miss my man. He was my first, my prince charming. He was there when I had nobody he brought me from nothing to something taught me, loved me, married me he was grea..."

"Well if he was so great why you kill his ass you forgot you the reason you mornin, he did so much for ya and YOU stopped his heart took his last breath."

"Jah why you gotta go there she know that."

"I'm just making sure cause every time we got our buzz going she come with that bull shit."

"Look just because I did what I did doesn't mean I didn't or don't love him sometimes we black out and can't control our actions and that's what happen to me as far as I'm concerned it's a street code and everybody should live by them and in my book he broke one of them. Why you shaking yo head?"

"I mean damn did you have to kill him? The nigga was gone die anyway" Jah said. These hoes crazy I thought.

"So you telling me some nigga infect you with AIDs you aint gone kill his ass or his rep? Hoe I can't even have kids without worrying if my baby is gone be a carrier I can't be in a real relationship people so ignorant to this disease. I don't even know how long a life I got to live and you telling me I'm wrong? No, I had a mutha fucken rite to take his, he took mine. So we even."

"You could of just left him, huh Mimi." Jah said under her breath

Chrys aint like that shit "Get the fuck out my house before I black out again hateful ass hoe." she screamed.

Jah wasn't expecting that cause she jumped a lil spilling a little of her drink "I'm looking at two killas but I'm hateful? I got money to make anyway" she said grabbing her purse and shoes.

As Jah took her time getting ready to leave I sat and thought about Chrys situation I feel where she coming from a nigga played with her life cause he didn't give a fuck about his own, didn't think about his future or hers. He had money he was some big time dope boy running tween Miami and Atlanta with Trigga City in the middle.

He had a son though I'm not sure how old he is now but had no other family except a homeboy he referred to as his brother a nigga in the dope game with him his right hand man. A nigga that's out here running loose, looking for Chrys ass as we speak to get revenge for his dawg. I'd probably kill him too he did basically take her life right from her, and she blindly killed him. Now she steady looking over her shoulder, wondering. Yet it all could have been avoided if she would have let him live maybe even got back together. It could of helped to be each other back-bone after time passed. That is what I'm guessing Jah is always trying to get her to understand. But Chrys see red when she mad don't hear nothing so she started up again.

"Hoe don't put her in it. She kill mother fuckers

that's already dead morally and spiritually. I did it cause I was M.A.D. Made A Dummy. Hurry up and get the fuck out my house and you moving hella slow money bags" Chrys yelled at Jah who was in the bathroom refreshing he make-up and look I assumed. I couldn't help but laugh the shit was funny and Jah didn't like that shit I could see in her eyes the way she glared at Chrys walking towards the door. Jah looked at me making the so gesture and rolling her eyes while shaking her head and shutting the door behind her. "I can't stand her sometimes. She be acting like she wanting somebody to knock her ass out, she like misery and everybody in it with her."

"Don't let her get you worked up you and Christopher Marlowe said it best *"Misery loves company"* and weed heads love weed fuck her I got some Cali bud."

She was pouring that nasty as Moscato and gestured me a glass knowing I hated that sweet shit. I declined. Fuck Jah she gotta be goin through some personal shit. She worried about other bitches and they shit, knowing shit will not and can't be changed.

I got real shit to think about like a pathetic man that assaulted me and the sorry man that killed the love of my life, my match. Two clowns on my list. A nigga they call A.P. he somewhere in Miami free after he took my baby life. And old ass Mr. Julius, Jen dad he probably was fucking wit her too. Stupid clowns out there got they life coming to an end soon I felt it. Fuck her shit she was on some petty shit what kind of person worries about how another person lives, a nobody, a person without a life, or a person mad at the world. Period.

*****

"Excuse me miss no need to run"

"Ain't nobody run... Oh hey what up doe? You stalking?"

"Come on now Tampa not that big at least that's what someone once told me."

"It's true, so what up?"

"Nothing on the way home. I was thinking bout you earlier today."

"So you thought me up huh?"

"Bout time too cause you sure wasn't going to call me."

"I just got a job been a lil busy and I know you understand that."

"Yea well I also understand all work and no play makes a dull Mina!" my gas stopped pumping.

"Yeah well you got my number call me and well set up a play date."

"Just promise you won't re-nig on me."

"Promise" I said closing my gas door and stepping inside my Benz "Call me tomorrow I got you."

"How bout I take you out right now, have you eaten? You can park your car next block ova and ride with me he said pointing at a gray 2011 Maserati Quattroporte parked in the corner. No one won't bother it you cool don't worry. I got a little clout around here. His ride was nice as hell he was nice as hell but as usual I had shit to do.

"I'm sorry bae, I'm on my way to work."

"Bae, I'm ya bae now? See I knew you want me."
Hell yea you mine! I thought "Damn now you can tell the future?"

"Hey what can I say a man of many traits. I guess I'll see your sexy ass around." he said walking off. I was on cloud nine just that little interaction with sexy got me high it's been so long since I meet a man I just wanted to be with and lawd I wanted to be with him right now. He was right though he had me at first glance.

When I pulled up to the club it was thick and it wasn't even nine o'clock yet. Yea tonight was gone be a good night I thought parking kind of towards the back so people can't associate my car with me I don't like everybody knowing my whip. Although I could associate they ass with they shit.

When you stepped in Hush Inc. go through the curtains walk in a couple feet you have two bars on each side of you about ten feet long. Looking straight ahead when walking in you got an oval shaped full liquor bar in the middle but closer to the end of the club. In the middle of the bar is a stage thirteen feet by ten that is specially used by veterans, the guest or host. An rectangular stage in the back of the club against the wall the main stage taking the width of the club with two doors on each side and two mini stages on both sides of you after the first two bars. Tables spread out all throughout the club so the angles where numerous.

To be honest HUSH had some of the baddest the bay had to offer. I done seen chocolate, red, yellow, black, even seen a cute thick white chick in there bitches got me asking myself, do I want to change up on the niggas but naw I need me a man at the end of the day. It's what was made for me, maybe I'll experiment one of these days who knows. Sexual tension is a mother fucker. Man I had been loving this job since I started it didn't really seem like a job to me at all I was partying and getting paid for it. I done seen some sexy ass men up in here I guess it's true they be all up and through the strip club white boys, college, business white and blue collar brothers. I worked a couple day time shifts when I first started but I guess I had night time appeal because I was there with em and it was OK with me I caught on quick I was fast I didn't mind moving how else did I keep this frame as firm as it was. I usually worked with one girl on my bar I was bar one it was in the front middle got a lot of traffic the most I guess because it basically the first bar you see. Tonight I was working with two other girls. Sammie a white girl pale with black hair and green eyes she was pretty just pale as hell two years older than me been at the bar three years her first bartending job. Gia an Arabic girl twenty eight been a bartender for seven years she was cool she talked a lot had a shit load of jokes but hey that's what bartenders do. We had two bar back a mixed kid and a Mexican they was real quite just did they job basically.

Come to find out Dave was not the shift manager he was the owner his little fresh ass no wonder he hired me so quickly without any hesitation or checking with anyone. He'd be upstairs in his office looking down at everybody he kind of reminded me of the beginning scene in "Belly". His office was up top at the end of the club a big glass wall for his viewing pleasure with blinds that hung over every opening. You could only get to his office through the dancers room or the fire escape exit to his room.

The homie Pablo comes here his ass come up here a lot I think he checking for this lil Jamaican beauty Kenya. Pablo's cool like a third father next to pops and Unk he the only one I trust outside family beside Jah, Lana, Chrys and my first taste of love Von before he was murdered. The loss of him really had me fucked up for a while, that shit really had me hating the world but after some years I got over it. I'm ready to really love again which takes me to Devontae I need to call that man back. Good lawd he is so sexy to me a Morris Chesnut version just taller but still beautiful smile *hmm*. I needed some damn customers before I nut behind this bar I thought. I began fanning myself and I happened to glance up and thought I'd seen Devontae sexy ass looking down on me but I was just trippin I had to have been cause I did a double take and he or whoever was gone. I needed some loving soon because my trips to Atlanta was not gone cut it I need some in-town love real talk.

*****

Today was nice as hell out I had to get out but I wasn't fucking with team crazy or new sexy today. I was waiting on my Boo my ace Lana. I had been waiting for a while when I was about to reach for my phone to call her I seen her sashaying her way to our regular table us four eat at in the cut. I waved and stood to embrace my Boo in a hug.

"Hey Ms. Boo."

"What up Me?"

"Me" was the name she gave me really short for Damina. I really didn't give a fucking care I liked it. If she said the name while telling a story nobody would know if she was talking bout a nigga or broad with that name. I called her Ms. Boo or Lana Boo I don't know why just did. Even though me Chrys, Lana, and Jah all met at the very same time and I spent a lot of time with the other two girls Lana was my dawg if you could pick out family by hand she'd be in the blood line, she thorough, kind of the last of the dying breed. If I didn't know her I swear she would be a mystery to me. Lana was Haitian bout 5'8, 127 pounds ten of those pounds was probably them big ass titties she had. Flawless black complexion, changing cat like eyes, full lips with bright smile and a natural mane that she was wearing straightened today. She was bad like me I loved the attention we got when we were together.

"So girl what's been up? I aint seen you since my birthday. Speaking of, what are you doing for yours next week?"

"Been working you know me. I need a vacation so I'll prolly dip, go disappear for a while."

"It's true, shit you and me both. We need to go somewhere where we can find all the men's girl."

"It's true, it's true, but I seen Tae on you at the club, somebody got they eye on the prey."

"He and I both Boo. Girl he so fine, what you know about him? Tell me something.

"He a nigga wit money, he calling shoots, no kids, he 25, he aint really with that bullshit, I heard bitches be stalking him."

"Girl stop playing."

"For real!" She had a serious ass face on but she wanted to laugh. I couldn't control myself the shit was funny, we had a good laugh then Lana ass got serious again. "I thank white girl decease boyfriend is his dawg I think he looking for her ass nobody told me that it's my own thesis just from knowing Chrys story and knowing enough of his. I'm pretty sure as a matter of fact so you might want to keep them apart one of them bound to recognize the other sooner or later."

Netta B.

# Chapter Sixteen

September 2012

"Hello?"

"Hey pretty girl."

"What you want?"

"Oh it's like that Mina?"

"Like what, what's up what you need something you OK?"

"Actually yes I need you, can I see you?"

"Yea around 1pm tomorrow I aint gone be doing nuthin."

"Damn like that Mimi?"

"Look I aint got time I can't do this right now."

"Can't do what? I just wanna see you."

"It's been a month since I seen you a week since I last spoke to you and we spoke less than a min I told you how I felt about you I really cared about you and you played me."

"Mina I know you got and had niggas in your face tryna lock in an..."

"But what do they have to do with what I tried to do with you? I tried to be with you. I felt a connection physically and mentally I wanted you. But now, I don't want shit from you. Not even your time which you never seem to have any for me anyway."

"I was tryna get us situated tryna get some money flowing you told me to stop that drop shit didn't you.

Look have you heard "Rock Star Swag" on the radio that's me. Winning that BET Freestyle Champion was a good look baby!"

"Well baby I glad to hear that, good for you Zaddy. Peace and blessings." That nigga had some nerve tryna talk to me and shit like everything was cool a nigga will run all up and through you if you let em, and I'm not the one I rather kill me a nigga literally. Talking bout "Rock Star Swag", nigga please. Right when I was reaching for my radio my phone rang again I know it's that nigga he must be feeling himself today well I had something for his ass.

"WHAT!"

"Are you gone always yell at me when I call? You the one who told me to call today." I smiled at the sound of the voice all frustration was far gone now.

"My bad you seem to call at the darnest times. What's up?"

"I mean come on today is the day, you said you had me today. I'm tryna set that play date up you ready to play lets go to a lounge I'll come get you round eight pm tonight."

"I don't know let me check my schedule."

"Naw I'm sorry baby but you can't check nothing you open I got your word yesterday."

I must admit I like how he was tryna take charge that shit turned me on aint to many strong minded men out here. "Oh really so what you tryna tell me Mr. Md.?"

"A min is too long Mina and you done had me waiting weeks, so just imagine how I feel."

"You better slow down you hittin that five point mark."

"Let me see you tonight so I can work the score board."

"Okay okay you got it, if you here at seven pm on the dot you'll get ten points added to your two."

"That's still not helping you'll still be in the lead by eight."

"Well where the extra eight points come from?"

"You agreed to the play date with me rite so that alone made you a winner."

"I aint mad at it. See you soon."

Man that Devontae be on his job, he best believe from here on out it's about to get a lot harder this just the pre-test. Getting with me and keeping me is the ultimate test all this shit that he doing to get me he better keep it up as long as we together he needs to live every day of his life like he tryna win me and I'll do the same thing to a certain degree I'm the lady so I gotta keep him on his toes make him wonder what I need, where I'm going, to keep me as happy as possible that's his job. Work provided no matter how much bank a lady got.

I took a shower, lotion my body with my mix oil, cocoa butter and Rhianna rebel, filled my eyebrows, applied mascara with a lil concealer for those puffy eyes and a poppin lip gloss. Ran the flat iron threw my tri color hair, and then slipped into my express sequin shorts and cute sheer shirt from cotton on with some cute lil booties from ALDO then slipped on my prescription ray bans. I was chillin today no purse I got pockets. I'll leave my keys and phone in his car. I had twenty minutes to waste so I went down stairs chairs to check out my bloodline.

"Man come on I know how to do the dance I seen it way before yawl jitts, you posed to be cool with it one nice smooth move yawl adding to much to it with all this hip shaking knee bending shoulder popping when Dougie Fresh did it was one cool and simple move."

"Who is Dougie Fresh?" C.J. said laughing at the name.

"The originator of that dance My Dougie he is a rapper probably bout my age that's his move all yawl kids now a days just copy all that we already done did from the movies songs dances to clothes so when I say been there done that I really mean it check this out." My dad started rappin lyrics and moving up and down like he rappin on a mic but that was not even the funny part while rapping he does his imitation of Dougie's dance my little brother went crazy with laughter when I stood behind dad imitating him I could barely do it I was laughing so hard but trying not to let my dad on to what was going on. When I calmed down I let my presence be known

"Oooo my Dougie! Dang CJ now I should probably stay home and really show you how to do it cause he kinda stiff"

"As yawl copy us grown stiff folks yawl gone get stiff too one day, so young in please." he said while doing the James Brown we all begin to laugh at that one

"Oww wee look at you girl you look just like your mother. Where are you going tonight Mimi?"

"I'm not sure my friend gone take me out get a lil loose."

"Loose? You mean what you just did right here rite? Let me tell you, you aint all that grown to be talking to me like that if you not."

"Naw since I been working I'm going out tonight since I don't have to work tomorrow off day relax day, he should be pulling up soon."

"Oh OK well the lucky little sorry ass boy aint coming to the door?"

"I told him not to I'm not ready for yawl meet and greet just yet." Right when I said that I see Tae pulling up

I looked at my watch and couldn't help but smile. I started walking towards the door. Eight minutes early, that's a good sign I thought. "Here he go pops I'll see you later love yawl. C.J. wont you teach dad how to jitt again put some of the "D" back in him help him loosen those bones."

"Oh so you real jealous of your old man huh?"

"Yessss" I said laughing.

It was so cute to see my daddy worked all up bout a man that right there showed me I'll always be his lil Mimi. I laughed at the thought while I went out the door. I couldn't even front I loved being daddies little girl. As I was walking out the door Tae was almost up to the door which proved to me maybe he was a true gentlemen and maybe letting him meet my daddy wouldn't have been so bad. That smile mixed with that walk made me give him an automatic hug.

"Finally!" he said which caught me off guard a little. He must have read the look on my face and said "I have finally touched you and you smell like a rebel now I just have to play out my fantasy of a kiss. So what's up pretty lady he said while slipping a kiss on my cheek." He reached to open the door.

"Well I guess you got two things off your check list and I am great I can't even complain and if I did I'd be dead wrong."

"Well I glad to hear that and to complain you would seem ungrateful" he said shutting the door. I reached and open his before he could reach it. "And that wasn't the kiss I was referring too." He said beginning to pull off.

I could tell tonight was gone be a good night I think I finally found one.

He pulled up to Berns Steak House, my favorite I have occupied their space here plenty of times on a lil me time tip I guess I could be called a regular and for him to just pull up here after making arrangements with me today for 9pm and me just telling him yesterday I could see him he had to be a regular also. He owned a carwash barbershop and restaurant. I was glad I aint come up on one of these "droppers" stupid ass niggas getting hold of a old ass hustle old ass crime and bringing it to a stop, why cause they aint never had nothing. I aint mad at em long as they stay from round me and my identity. I just wish they could be smart save that shit grow that shit niggas act like they can't flip money from what I hear you get thousands of dollars at a time, man give me a year, a season of what I can get then it's off to the flipping part of it. But people stupid well not stupid but greedy then again I guess greedy is stupid they just don't care. I'm glad I aint have to worry bout this nigga being creep round me tryna steal information and shit. I loved niggas on my level but I was really hoping he was above and beyond. We got a little private room which was cool cause I wanted to pick his head and see if he could pick mine.

"Girl you are looking lovely almost as good as my wife."

"Wife oh hell..."

"Let me finish, my wife Pam Grier I love a fighter and I can tell you are that you've done gave me challenges so now if your bank account match hers you can be wifey I'll dump her right now."

"Well if it's like that, if your bank account is like my ex Warren Buffet I'm willing to play wifey." shit who I'm kidding I was willing to play wifey the first time I seen this nigga at the gas station.

"OK you got me. I aint Buffet but if you can pull a big fish like that you are my soul mate all I got to say is if you stick around Damina we gone make some big moves beyond being hood rich. I see something in you I know OGs when I see one and I hope you do too. So with that being said let's make a toast to a blooming friendship a friendship because that's how love starts!"

"Cheers to that."

"So what's up? Tell me about Damina, everything that I need to know."

"I'm not the kind of girl to just tell, you gotta just do you if I like it I'll stick around if I don't, and well you know how it goes."

"Damn I knew it was a OG present. Since you put it like that I see you on some other type level definitely a grown woman about business. I can see you been hurt plenty of times or one major disappointment so it's a big strong shell up under a soft sexy structure. I wanna know you and help you. I know you don't need it but I wanna give it and receive it and I know you got support strength and a lot of love to give. I feel it already been seen it."

"Damn. You puttin it down rite now aint you just layin it all out. Huh?"

"Look I can respect that so...I can't even front I'm feeling you and what you speaking but I really can't answer your question. I'm just me I learn you, you learn me, words don't mean nothing to me it's all about actions. Everybody that got something, I mean really own something had to prove something. So I don't talk I just do me. My granddaddy use to tell me "you just like a lighter going bad people gotta be gentle but fast with you in order to get the flame. They gotta be fast because you don't play games you want the facts up front. What do they want from you? How will it benefit you? And gentle because you're a diamond your rare not many girls built like you. You are going to go through so much before you see your victory and baby girl your day will come as long as you stay true and focused to what you want." So that's all me I don't have to tell you nothing you know if you want me for life or just a night by observing me and in the first 15 min or our very first conversation. I'm just riding and if I want to get off I will and right now I'm enjoying the ride."

"I knew it, pretty girl OG."

*****

Over the last couple of days we were inseparable when I had the free time. We had been getting along great. He was a gentleman, a thug, a business man, a hustler. A man of his work and words. One thing I hated unmotivated liars. He was dedicated I liked how he looked you straight into your eyes when he talked to you and expected the same in return. I learned so much about him through his stories.

He liked to talk, to me at least, because he never stopped. I learned his mother was killed when he was five a burglary turned rape. She was suffocated. He and his dad had just went to go pick a pizza from Pizza Hut because they didn't deliver in the neighborhood. And it was forty minute drive there and back more or less. I figured somebody had their eyes on his mom because that's a very short window. At age eight his dad went to prison for manslaughter. Seems he had a vengeance. Tae went to go live with his aunt, who's boyfriend took Tae under his wing as a runner slash look out guess he thought Tae to be loyal and useful gave him his own block so on so forth. Tae got special treatment from his uncle he was like the son he'd never had. He wanted him to be street smart and respected in the streets but also wanted him in school getting that smart people language and business ethic down. He went to a community college studied business and management then went to a trade school barber school at age twenty by twenty one opened his first business then second, third so forth. Now he was twenty six his birthday just passed a week ago and was the crème of the crop boo had it going on, a sexy chocolate business man and he was all mine.

I wanted to show him off to the girls bad. I just aint want nobody to die. I don't know how but I had to intertwine my girls wit my nigga so they could be looking out for me telling me if any funny shit going on I'm sure it never will be but you never know.

Netta B.

# Chapter Seventeen

October 2012

**Antonio Preston**
**Age: 31**
**Race: Black**
**Height: 5'9**
**Weight: 162**

**Address: 1267 Pioneer Rd.**
**South Beach Miami Fl. 36781**

**Employment: CEO, boss**
**Hobbies: basketball games, strip clubs, kick boxing**
**Interest: performing arts, martial arts,**

Antonio Preston alias AP, Slimm is a multiple business owner. Cartel MAE (Money Aint Enough). Played basketball overseas France for three yrs. lives alone ladies man no kids mom dad three sister in St. Pete Fl. uses his status as a mentor to molest children young boys.

# Expired
## Completion call 8185555187 ext. 187

Here we go again another challenged individual who don't have or listen to his conscious. I mean how many people don't know right from wrong or just refuse to do right because they're too weak? To many for me that's for damn sure. I'm after someone new but for similar dumb ass reasons every time I turn around. I do love these flights though a time to relax I can be whomever I want to be or not. Being so high up in the air no worries just ride for a hour the least.

Today I was on my way to Miami, South Beach I couldn't wait it had to be at least two yrs. since I been there and that was to come clean up some twin brothers that molesting and targeting high school girls and boys. That was one of the most challenging cases because I had to get them alone at separate times which made it a little difficult. I acted like a set of twins that came on a summer vacation to visit our auntie, acting as if we didn't want be together on our vacation. I played a different roll for each twin never agreeing to a double date. It took six days exactly, very tiring.

This time I'm looking for an Antonio Preston. Now this Antonio was too damn fine to be bout to die one of the top hustlers started his own little cartel out here in Miami bout five yrs. ago. He all over Florida Georgia and Texas wit it but he official, a thorough nigga came from nothing but in the mix of a good breed. Graduated high school and college has a full service barbershop on Miami Beach, kind of a man spa. Didn't have kids the oldest of four, and was out here getting to it. Unfortunately for him he was a fuck-king fag round here touching on little ass boys. His fetish is lil virgin boys like really who does that? A man tearing down another young man it's sad. He could pick a woman high on the pedestal because of how he presents himself, as well as his empire he built himself with legit businesses hiding the real life he would be any woman dream. But hey it's his life his choices. He just made it easier for me. His nasty ass ways brought his ass right to me....sweet vengeance for Javon. Number two about to be marked off man 2012 may really be my year.

This was too easy I found Antonio just by quenching my thirst a light flirt at the bar which led to dinner that next night, to dessert at my place the next night well not my place a red headed big goggle glasses wearing girl that goes in and out of this room.

Antonio came to the room two minutes early a man about his business I see good thing I cracked it open a few minutes head of time didn't want the cameras to get glimpse of the real me after his knock I chimed in its open. Antonio came in looking oh so dapper in his dark cream suit off white collar shirt and the perfect little handkerchief with banging ass Stacie Adams I won't even get on the accessories but one piece a jewelry man it was one piece I couldn't help but notice and compliment. We exchanged hellos I excused myself to the restroom and room service with the food came right as I shut the bathroom door excellent timing once again.

During our meal I began my heavy flirting and a lot of pouring I wanted him tipsy but I didn't want him out of it. I knew since our second and last meeting that he was the A.P. I was looking for he told me how he lived in Tampa a while back played basketball for varsity but was also doing what he could on the streets just in case. He told me a story, said he owed somebody debt and had to pay, no way around it. After he payed his debt he felt he had to get out of town and moved to Miami seven yrs. ago stayed with some uncles or some shit. He never said what he did what was his debt he just said every war has a casualty and any casualty can cause a war. That shit was deep and kind of speaking his fate if you thought about it. Shit I knew he was the one I had been looking for, him telling his story the guilt in his eyes told it all.

"You want another drink Antonio bout to make me another"

"Dang girl you swimming through those drinks let me find out you tryna take advantage of me." he said while tryna get up off the love seat "I gotta use the bathroom when I come back you better have something for me."

"Yes sir" I said with a smile I walked over to him asking him to unzip my dress knowing I could do on my own but wanting him to feel like he was really running this. While he was in the bathroom I slipped off my dress to reveal my matching set pulled out a chair handcuffs and feathers and whip cream had to set up my stage. He came stumbling out talking bout "Damn girl you fine ass fuck that's what I'm talking bout. Yea I'm finna make you mine you ever balled with a baller."

"No but I teach ballers."

"Well come teach me something."

"Come sit right here" I said pointing to the chair soon as he sat down and was straighten up to look at me I knocked his ass out with the butt of my gun. I grabbed the belts to the robes tied his feet to the chair cuffed his hands behind the chair then duct tapped his mouth. Put on some jeans a baby tee my retro's and tied my hair up. Antonio was different I couldn't just kill him I had to torture him let him know he dying cause he killed my best friend and how I caught up with him was because he a nasty fuck. I grabbed my gun and began cleaning it thinking about the night Javon gave it to me, it was a little girly gun a NAA Guardian I guess he wanted me to have something tiny and concealable. He must of left it at the house the night of my birthday because I found it the next night while taking a smoke break to figure out and ponder my move on my very first assignment the high school chick who was a scuba instructor assistant. It was in a Tiffany and Co box on the card it said.

*We all grow, learn, and die but very few live... As long as you do what you want to be doing you living!*

*Love, Always*
*VON*

It had a pearl handle and at the bottom of the clip it said "Wifey" that message right there let me know he loved and accepted me that told me he didn't care what I did or what anyone else thought of it at the end of the day I was his, his wifey. That alone made me feel like I owned this right. The little time and memorizes of him made me feel like I at least owe him this. I would seek whatever vengeance he had.

I got tired of waiting for dookie dick to wake up so I woke him up myself gave him a few slaps in the face. "Hey doodoo you up, you have nice little rest?" Sorry but I had to wake you up so we could get this shit over with. I got a few questions. Seven yrs. ago in Tampa was that body that was in the alley way of Nome Dr. the reason you ran, didn't want a body case to deal with?" his eyes shot open then he started going all berserk "So I guess it is true huh? Next question did you kill him over debt or did you try him and he wasn't wit that fuck boy shit?" He shook his head no I aint know whether to believe him or not. "OK I believe you. Now, third question and thirds times a charm. Why the fuck do you molest on little boys these kids trust and look up to you do you know how sick of a person you have to be to do shit like that?" He noticed my gun on the table cause he started going crazy guess he thought he was gone loosen some shit up, but no sir not my military knots. I was sick of him he was a murdering down low brotha and he was about to be exposed so first I went around his back and stabbed him in it "Watch cha back you can't trust everybody." I did that first because I figured that's how he got Von stuck him in his back first while he was walking away aint no way a nigga got up front first. I watched him squirm a little then walked in front of him. He looked so sad like he wanted to say something like he needed to tell me something or maybe I just wanted to hear an explanation. I pulled one end of the tape off.

"I'm sorry but it was him or me. Who wouldn't do it just out of fear alone? I didn't want to die I was too young."

"Don't give me that shit. What about him he was young he wanted to live."

"Yea but he was quite he didn't do too much of nothing. He didn't ball wasn't going to college. He aint have a future. My life been bomb I done gave back grew learn and shared som…" I covered his mouth back up I couldn't take another insult about my heart. I just looked at him for a minute. I couldn't believe he felt what he done was justified. I stabbed him in his gut blood started dripping down his mouth his eyes were pleading please stop but I can't read the sorry language. I knelt down in front of him unzipped his pants and searched for his dick in his pissy and shitty pants. Which almost made me throw up but I aint leaving any incriminating mess behind. When I found it I pulled it out and smiled looking up at him and to think it felt like this niggas dick jumped in my hand he actually has the audacity to feel a little pleasure I thought, filled with anger and disgust before I knew it I had my knife to his dick here he go still thinking my fine ass gone please him when the proof states otherwise. With my knife to his dick I said this is for the boys who hold your secrets I sliced that little two inch piece of wrinkled up meat off so easily I felt like Lorena Bobbitt. With him carrying on like I just killed him I went ahead and killed him but not before expressing myself.

"I loved Javon he was somebody to me and his future was with me." I tighten my grip on the knife and completed one last puncture wound to his heart. I had to puncture it because he punctured mine. And just like that me my baby and those boys could finally rest.

*****

January 2013

"Waking up to bed in breakfast. Word baby what this lil surprise for?" It smelled like it was about to go down. "Let me sit up straight so I can digest everything." I said fixing a space to put the plate on my lap.

"Baby I'm feeling you so much you like my other half we think the same want the same out of life....success. After these last couple of months all I see is love, you been a real friend I really wanna spend my life with you building. I think, naw I know it's love."

"Oh that's sweet but damn that's a lot to take in I

just woke up five minutes ago do you need a answer now."

"I need something. Do you feel the same? Don't leave me hanging Mina"

"I mean I wouldn't leave you hanging you deserve more." I took a slight pause "Well baby, to put it in lamest terms...I love you too!" I said cheesing planting a kiss on his cheek. "But I just don't know about the spending the rest of your life part."

"Oh you Dave Chappelle lil sister now?!"

"No but I'm Rich bitch!"

"Oh OK watch ya mouth that's not how a lady talks. But for real I trust you and wanna share my world with you I also got a great opportunity I think may be great for you I've been looking for the girl for a while and now I know I've found her in you."

"Well what is it baby you know I got yo back I know you will not put me in dangers way."

"Let me find out."

"Find out what?"

"I found me a gangtress."

"What you thought an OG was."

"What is that noise?"

"What? I don't hear nuthin."

"Sound like a phone but there go our phones."

"Hold up!" I ran to my purse fumble threw and found what I was looking for "Oh it is my phone. Hey Dad." I said throwing a smile on and pointing at the phone for Tae

"I'm good just with T. Well I can probably do that for you today dad let me see what T got planned which I don't think is anything if I can't do it today I promise I'll see you and take care of it tomorrow." When I turned around Tae was not sitting anymore he was standing right in my face. I liked the fact that this phone just made him show his true colors now I see he not the one to be played with and that was good to know cause like I said before I'm definitely not the one, I will kill his ass before I let him hurt me. "What's wrong baby." I said reaching for him

"What the fuck! Where the fuck did that phone come from and why I don't got that number."

"This is my phone for my dad only I don't even know this number by heart it's a prepaid phone I'm never on it unless pops call me."

"Do I look stupid what you got going on where you got two phones you got another man?"

"OMG. look my dad got me this cause he know how my moods change I don't feel like being bothered and I will cut my phone off in a heartbeat. This is just so he'll always be able to get through to me, and if that was my man I was just talking to he a lame as nigga for being so calm and not asking me where I been spending all my time at. Chill out that was my dad you my daddy."

"Yea OK I gotta watch you girl you got game I know it you always got your poker face on."

"And you are always watching the chess board." I said just to throw some shade his way "Everything not a chess game, some shit as easy as checkers." Because of the ugly look on his face I changed the subject "So you gone give me the details of the lick or nah? Oh you mad now and gotta reshuffle ya deck?" I laughed. He looked at me like he was about to strangle my ass then laughed a little to himself.

"You tryna call me a baby on the slick huh it's OK it's cool. So look, I overheard a conversation between my boss man and this sick ass crooked fool Rich. I despise that man and I need you as bait with your looks, charm, and VERY little to no good ass sex I know he'll tell you any and everything because he likes to feel important and in control and if it's in you set it up so I can kill his ass."

"OK I'm sure you have your reasoning for wanting to cross and or even kill this Rich dude but you sure you want to cross your boss? Pablo is cool and it seems like yawl close to you sure you don't wanna think a little about it? Or instead of leaving with all the shit when you can just take it back to Pablo and yawl split the profits I can tell he loves you like family."

"I'm tryna make us rich and if I keep working for Pablo. I aint gone never get over the hump this is a big as lick and why you worried about Pablo you don't even know that nigga. I'm yo man and whatever I say I want to do or going to do you should be right behind me telling me baby you can and will get it done. Plus Pablo aint got no money tied to this I'm clear he won't lose."

"You right I'm sorry. and Tae, you can and will get it done with me behind you." and it was true I loved this man straight up he just didn't know how down I was and as long as he always holds me down and was for me as far as I was concerned we even. But I'll give Pablo the money he would of made I got so much money need to get rid of some of it and if it'll keep him and Pablo clear I'm willing to do it.

PRETTY: Her Introduction

# Chapter Eighteen

Tae was getting on my damn nerves we been going over this shit like all morning long, and now he was on my damn phone still talking while I was driving to the Starbucks to seek Mr. Bad ass Rich but I sat and listen again like the submissive little woman all men wanted.

"OK baby you remember what I told you rite. Be soft, sweet, innocent, eager, young dumb..."

"Yea yea. He likes em young naive black and fine. I got it baby don't worry." I said hoping he would get off the damn phone and luckily it worked. Pulling up it was the normal half full, half empty Starbucks scenario the thing about doing jobs at home is anyone can recognize you and I really didn't want to deal I been thinking hard about this. I wanted to just appear younger dress wise I wore glasses and a lot of people did not know that, I hated em. I figured while dealing with him I would I added hair pieces in my hair even though my hair flowed way past my shoulders it again was to add appeal. Today my style of dress the classic school girl look I was rocking a fitting knee skirt high school sweatshirt I cut to fall off my shoulders some really cute booties heels from bakers big bamboo hoop earrings that read "bad" and a high messy ponytail. When I went in I went in signing the song that was on my iPod which was a song called "Refill" perfect song to make a scene if you ask me I went in there smiling and signing walking myself up to the register to order "can I get a reefiillll, can I get a reee-eee-eeee-ee......" I did a couple of hip sways and booty pops while at the counter ordering when I turned around I had a few audience members including Rich but I was catching the back of his head as he turned back to his table. There was a table cater-corner to his that was perfect I went to go sit my things on the table and have a seat until my order was called. On the way from the counter from picking up my order one of my audience members was feeling himself because his scrawny geeked out ass was smiling and walking straight up to me

"Hey pretty lady you dining alone." He caught me off guard with that one his old crusty pale self was about to put the game down. I would have normally let him go ahead and do him just for laughs but I was on mission and wondered what Rich was doing right now and if he was watching me. I zoomed back into my attacker, looked down at my feet then back up to him. I sighed.

"I don't think that's a good...." when someone cleared their throat behind me I was about to step to the side to let them pass when I realized who it was I couldn't help but smile "Oh, there you are." I looked back to Mr. Aggressor "Well see I was about to tell you I was waiting on someone." it wasn't the total truth but he aint have to know that. "Maybe next time cutie"

"If your ever so lucky, I'm a be gone by then little lady" the man said throwing his hands up and walking off.

"Or maybe not..." I laughed while turning to look at Rich. Looking at him now he was clearly a handsome man he didn't look white though like Tae said he was and he had a familiar look his eyes kind of froze me a little.

"Well thank you Mr.?"

"Oh please no Mr. just Rich. Miss?"

"Juno! No misses on mine either." I added trying to add more innocence and gullibility to the situation.

"Sweet little Juno" he smiled motioning for me to sit and I did adding a thanks and a giggle. "So are you new to town a high school student?" and it worked he became a little too eager

"Well I just became a free woman I just graduated and turned eighteen last week and hopefully moving into my big sisters place this weekend."

"Oh they can't be that bad" he was sitting right in front of me now looking me over then into my eyes, which made me a little uncomfortable."

"Who can't be?"

"Well your parents of course."

"How'd you know?" I played along.

"You seem...I just can tell....honey they were just trying to protect you"

"I don't know why I'm a big girl."

"It's what parents do, if I was your daddy I wouldn't let anybody touch you, I'd be on you all the time." He said with a blatant devious smile.

"I can protect myself."

"That I am sure but there are plenty of perv's out preying on pretty young tenders like you. See Juno you have to have someone you can trust out here, a friend if you will. It's hard but you must find one these days..." he was making everything so easy he bought himself to me on the first day of seeing me he's laying it on thick too. He wants to be my friend. It's crazy how people act for pussy but even a little sicker what they'll do to steal or trick someone out of their innocence.

"Luckily I've found a friend in you to serve and protect. I said batting my little eyes with a smile. I'm not sure if I told you thank you for that interception you did earlier I think you saved me from one. "

"I try my best."

*****

Meeting Rich was kind of eerie I felt like he reminded me of someone. I just couldn't remember I'd have to figure it out later. I had to go see what Pablo had up his sleeve. Money time.

"Mimi! Baby girl how you doing they treating you good over at Hush Inc. every time I see you look different what is this look you rocking and how is that lil knuckle head Devontae treating you?"

"I'm good Low I can't complain. I try to stay looking good with all that money you done hooked me up with I don't have no reason not to. I'm loving that job over there some of the people I meet at that bar are what I need to make my days go by quicker and enjoyable and as far as that knuckle head he the reason for the get up."

"What the fuck? He like little girls got fetishes and shit got you dressing like this? Damn it's crazy how you know so little about your main man. I'm surprised you still fucking with him."

"Naw. No it's not like that; evidently like you he done seen something in me and think I'm the key to the perfect heist. He tryna sick me on somebody and I just left from quote unquote meeting him. And he likes them young."

"Oh ok. Thank god. I knew it was a reason I liked that boy. Mina you almost scared me thought I was gone have to get some new friends. So who he sic-ing you on? What the lick read?"

"Now you know I don't do business like that, and speaking of business, what's ours?"

"A true business woman. Here is all his info and pictures half the money too. I need this taken care before the end of next month he been moving and jumping states a lot tryna stay out of radar. A smart stupid nigga."

"OK I got you Low um I wanted to tell you I thinking about calling it quits on this murk-in shit I don't want to go to hell or die tryna execute a plan. I want a regular life with kids' stuff like that. Tae was mad as hell when he heard my other phone ringing I was worried he would take it and look at the number or something. Don't get me wrong I don't want to seem unappreciative. I'm grateful I mean you letting me be a part of your organization and keeping it business I'm just tired I aint gone never find that fool that tried to rape me back in the day that's what I was feeding off but that demon is dying."

"Mimi you owe me no explanation just a referral to somebody is all I ask cause I don't know where I'm a find a replacement for you. Come here give me a hug you family girl I got yo back my lil brother Von loved you, and you know Unk did even more and I do too. Do what you feel is right no matter what it is or who it affects. Nobody takes care of you like you can take care of yourself."

"Thank you Pablo I'll be in contact." He reminded me of Javon so much. They daddy must have been the ultimate player they were so much alike it was ridiculous.

PRETTY: Her Introduction

# Chapter Nineteen

That song by Musiq and India Arie Chocolate High is how he made me feel he just didn't know or maybe he did if he didn't propose to me I strongly felt like I would be the one on the knee I want a family the whole shebang snotty bad ass kids and all I don't need and want for anything but that companionship. He better not try to fuck me over on this lick only using me to complete an task because I will kill his ass my heart is not to be played with it has already been through too much. When I do this for him I'm retiring. I sat thinking while riding to Tae parents' house. He said he was looking for some pictures or something he was trying to figure something out and he wanted to take a trip to Miami said it was business and I wasn't going straight like that.

We pulled up to his moms and dads house, it went to him when he turned eighteen it was his get a way. The house was off MLK it was a nice little four bedroom flat green in color one of the nicest house on the block it's up keep and maintenance was well taken care of. He had a ugly little cat in the yard he was talking to I hope he kept that shit outside, last thing I needed was a sneaky ass cat staring and walking round me. In his room he had sports equipment, trophies, books, and cd's everywhere. I could tell he came here a lot it wasn't dusty as it should've been. He came sat on his bed where I was with two big photo albums and a box full of pictures. Whatever he was looking for he was serious.

I took a hand full of pictures not looking for anything really but ready for a roast session if I came across something that was too much and couldn't be left alone. So far he was in the clear he was a cute ole chubby baby with a head full of hair. His mom was light skinned she was pretty and they had the same ears and smile, but he looked like a spitting image of his dad, twins. Seen a couple high school pictures of him in his uniform or posing with who he said were cousins. Came across a couple of girls he was hugged up on, they were all beauty queens badd just like me. The next picture I seen was a jaw dropper I stared at the picture for a min trying to put together what I was looking at when it hit me like a knife to the heart I took a deep breath.

So now I was sleeping with the enemy? In my fucking hand was not only the key that could make Tae hate me but it was also the confirmation that Lana was dead on about Chrys and her own personal dilemma. No wonder why she thought Tae looked familiar at AJA that night, probably too drunk to realize death was closer than she thought. Not only was this an old ass picture of Chrys ex but it also was Antonio or A.P. the nigga that I had just murked out in Miami a while back ago. I don't know how long I stayed there staring at that picture before I moved to the next one.

"So who's this I seen a few of your friends but I aint never seen him and this is the only picture of him I see in here was he your brother." I asked him who Chrys man was first which I knew and was pretty positive by his reaction he aint want to talk about it. Shit I didn't even want to talk about it I done seen his face so many times and ended so many good nights on bad notes because of this guy. "I'm sorry I don't mean to be nosey or anything but it's not too many pictures with you and niggas in here so who is he?"

"That's my homie my Ace from back in the day and why you say was like you know he passed or something?" "I don't know it's kind of an old picture, I don't mean to jinx death on anybody. I'm sorry." I chimed in as fast as I could.

"Naw you good. He gone his rotten bitch killed him I don't know why either they say she moved to Canada. I don't know but if I ever see her boney ass again she meeting her maker." *For one she damn sure isn't boney anymore some would say she a little chunky.* "Damn don't look scared I aint gone hurt you it's just a sensitive subject to me he was family for real you know how Big Meech all about loyalty and family well that's how we got down family for life. I'm just mad his life was shortened at such a fucking young age leaving his son behind without a father; every boy needs a real man in life. So yeah that's where I come in you remember Cam? That's his son my lil homie he straight though, long as I out here. But, I don't want to talk about that right now that shit really do not matter not now."

I moved on to on the other face Antonio I brought him up on a little lighter note. "Well…where he at? I aint never seen him my home girl would like him." that peaked his brow a little bit and got his attention.

"Oh that nigga dat's my homie he out in Miami then his chest soften a little well he was in Miami he just passed away a couple months ago around the same time you was in MIA. He basically the reason I'm going out there. I'm tryna member places and faces we use to see while we was out there. I haven't talked about it because I tryna still believe it, you don't know my nigga he been everywhere done all type of shit and know a million people. I just don't understand what happened, or why it happened. I can't even see it happening he was a real nigga, fuck that a real man. A mentor to me, and I was the older one. Bae they cut his fucking dick off, who cuts...I mean who deserves to get they dick cut off."

I just held him I didn't know what to say my heart was pounding fast and hard I wonder if he felt it and what was he thinking because I was thinking guilty your honor. I wish he knew I wish I could tell him but he wouldn't understand hell he wouldn't believe the truth, he had too much respect for the man. A dream turned fucking nightmare, when shit gets real. I'm sleeping with a fucking enemy part 2. Tae gone kill me or Chrys shit or us both. How can something so right turn out to be so wrong? I mean yea Ms. Boo told me bout Tae looking for Chrys that aint really my problem and he don't have no proof to think I would know that she was who he was looking for. That was easy but not now. Now I'm on his list and he don't even know it and I can't ever let him find out. I had to finish our business and end it somehow.

Tae think we gone follow Rich and get all in his business by me being the snake for a whole yr. I agreed to do that when he proposed this to me, but that nigga crazy if he think I'm follow this man all around like that, aint nobody got time for that a whole year shid in my mind I would do this two months the max and it's been like three or four, and both of them was erkin my nerves. I don't see how people deal with two and three lovers at a time. But that was not my real issue I had to get away from Tae I could no longer be with him forever I feared what he might do if he found out I killed his friend putting two and two together with me being gone around the date of his death or thinking I'm linked somehow here to trap him or something would straight kill me enough I wouldn't even need his bullet. It was time for me to put matters in my own hands.

*****

"So girl how you been you all hemmed up leavin me and Jah to kill each other with the occasional appearance of Lana, aint love beautiful?" Chrys said looking like she wanted to hear a story. She needed some love in her life. Tonight we were doing one of our girls day but Lana was absent I was really kind of hoping she would be here I just didn't get a chance to call her ahead of time. She was at the last girl day I missed it though.

"Girl I guess." I said waving her off. "I mean, hell yea!" I said laughing "And not only is it beautiful it's an in home chef, masseuse, butler, and most importantly dick. Yes love is a beautiful thing." I said looking for somebody to high five me Jah finally did. With a whatever behind it. I wasn't bout to start with her so I started talking mainly to Chrys. "So member the dude from the club that's who I been with Tae.

"Oh OK Mr. Dom Perignon I thought I knew him but I don't know nobody named Tae I guess he just got one of those faces."

"Actually you may know him he knew Denocka said he was real close to him he got a picture of them in his crib told me if he ever caught the bitch that killed him she breathe her last breath that's another reason I never brought him around I don't know if he'll recognize you."

"For real do you know if he goes by another name?"

"He told me Bricks when we first met."

"Bricks?!?" She said with wide eyes "Oh shit it is him yes keep him far away keep him under wraps you got pics of me anywhere don't..."

"He aint been in my room and as long as I live wit

pops it'll never happen."

"What a never happen?" Jah jumped in the conversation out of nowhere. "Yall in the same fucking city. What you jumping for looking like Casper all spooked and shit, you been known this nigga out here looking for you." then she faced me "And you, I aint think you was gone make it out here between your new job and secret boyfriend can't nobody meet up with you, you always tired and everythang thought you was gone leave us hanging like always, I aint feeling you today."

"Well I'm here as you can see, yall are and will forever be my Boo's." I said to Jah then put my attention back to Chrys. "Lana know him she gave me the ups on him, and I know yall aint in the same social circle. You good."

"Yall retarded." Jah said it low but loud enough for us to hear.

"Lawd, girl don't start this gone be peaceful night." Chrys said

"I'm just saying"

"Dang must we always argue in this bitch you got to take your trick problems elsewhere." Chrys stayed calling her a hoe.

"No, please Jah speak yo mind. I mean let's just get it all out we've known each other to long. We adults, we should be able be civilized about everything." I said

"Well why you walking round here all happy rich and shit act like shit don't get to you?"

"Are you serious you mad cause I be smiling? Girl stop." She was looking serious like bitch you aint answer my question I'm waiting.

"Dang Jah you miss me huh?" I smiled a lil still she aint budge I was getting heated now this bitch tripping I wasn't gone act up though I'm a use my polite voice and see what's really hood if this bitch jump or not but if she really wanted a answer here goes. "When you smile at someone don't they automatically smile back it's all about respect you walk and talk how you want people to perceive you walk with your head up high walk with a mission and they can't help but wonder who you are or what you do. You are the main factor in determining your future you bring the positive and negative energy in your life you can't blame it on others whether they build you or tear you down they only can do as much as you let them. I read this book the Four Agreements and it helped me on how I approached and receive people."

"Chile boo. Ain't nobody tryna hear that mess you aint shit just like me I fuck for money and you kill for the shit which is a little bit higher on the sinner score board. I don't know how you got mixed up in that shit and I don't care just stop walking round wit ya nose and chest all high and mighty like yo shit don't stink cause I can smell it miles away."

"First I walk and act how I want people to perceive me and second I know what I do and walk with my own demons and if I feel like either of you two tell my secret I'll..." I looked over at Chrys who was looking kind of scared maybe more so shocked either way her look kind Of brought me back before I said some crazy shit "See I aint gone take that personal I'm a smile and say I love you and turn the other cheek you really mad at yourself not me something else the book taught me. I love you chicka. I'll call yawl later. Jah you better check yourself life can be short." I said then shut the door I heard her start yelling but I don't know what that hoe said she aint come outside or call me so she must didn't want me to know. A warning, threat, promise, or clue shit she could take it how she wanted.

*****

"Juno your such a sweet girl, and we've been spending a lot of time together since you keep your apartment a secret I want you to take my penthouse and stay right here in the heart of downtown if you agree here is your key. I know I'm rarely here or in town and you stay with your sister so this will give you the alone time that you need and the privilege for me to see you whenever I want."

"For real thank you baby my own spot at 18 you putting the spot in my name right?" Rich looked off then shook his head

"Yea, if that's what you want baby girl."

"Oh this the bomb birthday present and it's not even my birthday that's what's up you really are my knight that serves and protect thanks fat daddy."

"No thank you pretty girl for putting up with an old man and always knowing what to say. Anything for you little girl, now for the RULES! First and last no man in my house, Point blank period!"

"Yes sir." I said planting myself on his lap and pecking him on the cheek. It hadn't even been a full month before he put me in a 2013 Porsche Panorama the only one in the Bay and had my name on the papers, said so I wouldn't ever complain about car trouble and now this Cracka tryna make me a house slave. Yea it was time to speed this up. Now he does just about give me anything I want I obey I stay smiling never question him and keep pieces of skin showing. Have not had to open the legs and have sex with him yet but I did play what he called student and teacher and let him spank me and play between my legs through my panties while I sit in a chair with my back to him which made him nut, I was amazed. He asked me to do a couple other deviant things which I will never repeat.

Me being who I am I've already memorized his codes to his gates house cameras safes everything, he uses two different codes. He makes sure I know his schedule down to the T cause he wants me around and waiting for him during his free time. I cook him dinners, give massages, and play his little games just so he don't stop talking he tells me about everything and everybody down to the very minute details. I just listen and take everything in I learn and hear then take it rite back to Tae.

PRETTY: Her Introduction

# Chapter Twenty

February 2013

**Andre Jones**
**Age: 23**
**Race: Black**
**Height: 5'9**
**Weight: 137**

**Address: 856 Sprucer Rd.**
**Atlanta, GA.**

**Employment: pharmacist**
**Hobbies: -------**
**Interest: -------**

**André Jones is a stealing clipping money and raped a girl who he did not know was the Don's sister daughter.**

**Expiration date: OVER DUE**
**Completion call 8185555187 ext. 187**

I was glad I was getting away I needed it. It had been

a stressful couple of days for me I didn't know what to do. I loved having Tae in my life but in reality we were enemies. I didn't see us being good for each other in the end. He was irritable, I was paranoid, I mean we still had that attraction but there were awkward silences or one would catch the other looking at them just watching studying. I was feeling like we were Mr. and Mrs. Smith. I was living on the edge in fear, a place I have never been to, I was uncomfortable and I didn't like the feeling. I didn't know what I was gone do I killed his friend his homie I know he can't connect shit to me so what if I was out of town in Miami that don't mean I killed him, but then again it's always something. I was sleep when it started but it wasn't a dream.

"Mina!" Tae said waking me up out my sleep

"Yes baby what's up what's wrong?" I jumped up trying to focus in on him standing on my side of the bed.

"Where you get this fucking ring from?" *Oh shit, why didn't I take that back to the house?*

"Um I got it when I was out in Miami. Some man pawned it to me I was looking for gold you know how I love jewelry and sometimes I find good deals at the pawn shops." *He aint buying it.* "How you found it? I was gone get it cleaned insured and stuff and give it to you."

He asked me all kinds of question what shop what the man look like that sold it what day did I get it. He woke me up out my sleep but I think I answered all his questions to his satisfaction. I was worried but for no reason because aint no way I would get caught up I could kill in my sleep and still clean all the evidence up. So police and all that other shit I aint worried about but Tae yea I'm worried about him he got all the evidence he need that ring. Maybe he would think Antonio sold it or lost it, and the upside to that is he couldn't confirm my story with the doodoo lover. So I was good, but yes this business trip was dually needed.

I had been watching this Andre dude for about three days now. He aint really do too much shit he was kind of still barely ever leaving out his apartment. I noticed he was a good Samaritan always helping folks so I figured I would implement that into my plan to bait him. It was around nine thirty a Thursday night, he was getting into his car probably getting cigarettes and beer one of the only reasons he would really leave. I followed him to a gas station to put me in his visual. Dre was walking back to his truck when he noticed and smiled at me. I smiled back and it was on from there. He hopped in his truck and rolled down his window starting off with a simple "Hey" I played along till I could throw in the bait. He couldn't wait to ask for my number and that was my cue to go fishing.

"This is so embarrassing to say. My man and I just had a fight earlier today he kicked me out and turned my phone line off. So I was tryna find a cheap little hotel/motel to stay in tonight but I don't got no damn phone to call around and I don't want to waste gas driving around. It was just nice to see a smiling face I had to speak to you."

"Dang ma..."

"I know right, it's my damn furniture he puttin his funky butt and big head on, he just pay everything. I got just as much right as he does being there. As far as I'm concerned about it, it's fifty/fifty when it comes to that spot."

"Damn come stay at my spot and save your money. Call ya man in the morning he prolly be done calmed down by then."

"For real and what you want, what you gone do?

You could be a killa."

"Come on now chill out do I look like a killa."

"Do I man?" He laughed but I held my straight face.

"Just by looking at you I know that man worried, I'm just tryna help. Follow me or not."

Now on the outside I was acting all scared and hesitant but on the inside I was break dancing. People just don't understand how easy it is to read some of they ass or just learn em in just a few hours or minutes of watching them. You people better switch it up every now and again. He lived in a decent apartment unit. One bed one bath, it was pretty empty inside to be honest it looked like a duck off spot, wasn't much of nothing in there but a radio, TV, bed, two couches and a folding table.

"You smoke?" he asked me

"I'll hit it for the occasion."

"What's that?"

"I met a special friend man."

"Hell yea that's a good enough reason for me." he said lighting a lil white boy up.

"So where you from again?" I asked tryna seem into him

"Illinois."

"Oh OK I know people up there."

"Word, who?"

"Damn you know the whole city?"

"I'm just saying."

"I may tell you later so tell me some more about you."

"Man I got bout 20 something siblings I'm the baby play football and base..." He started but I soon faded out I aint give a fuck bout this nigga. I had one more Mina offender out there and I felt like I was on his ass I felt it in my bones. *"I miss her but at least I got you around to help me remember her. Do you want a real daddy?" "I got a real fucking daddy, get off me" "Calm that shit down. I'll kill your ass nobody know we together....I lied....Shut up don't move or I will cut your as..."*

"Net. Net! Damn you there girl, day dreaming on me or something? You ok?"

"Oh my bad, thinking of that fuck nigga I'm all messed up right now."

"I understand not too long ago me and my old lady..."

"I don't mean to cut you off but I need to unwind can I take a shower real quick? You can get in to help wash my back."

He aint even answer me he just got up ran the shower, got naked in the bathroom then came out walking all around the room butt naked turning on music turning up the heater doing shit people who know they about get some do. I didn't care I wanted to get back to my room I didn't feel like playing tonight he was too easy and gullible anyway.

"Net you coming?"

"Yea um Dre I'm kinda shy so I'm a cut off the light" I said showing half my body that was naked so he wouldn't worry. I flicked off the light then made my way to the shower sliding in the back of the shower. Just like a nigga he all up in front directly under the water. I hated getting in the shower with niggas unless we was fucking other than that separate please.

"Baby where you at?"

"I'm right here you feel me?"

I hugged him from the back with one hand, rested my chin on his back then whispered in his ear. "Dre? Messiah said you wouldn't be able to run forever, and stop chasing pussy it don't love you it's three out of five men downfall!" When he turned to look at me or do whatever it was he thought he was about to get off I shot dead in his face with my sawed-off shotgun.

*****

"Hey bae what's up I'm missing the fuck out of you."

"What's up girl, why you think I'm calling? I feel the same."

"Aww. I'm not doing nothing just now closing this property out for my mom's I'll be back in town tomorrow"

"You just now closing the deal?"

"Well sealing it drinking eating kind of the celebration of future business partner type thing."

"I got it so that's how you stay fresh huh that real-estate money?" he said with a slight giggle. "Well, I'm out here in Miami just trying to find some more information out on Antonio I know somebody know something tryna go by what you told me and the info you gave. This my second friend that's been slaughtered and I don't know if I can live and not get justice for them I feel I'm obligated."

"Baby I'm sure you'll find all the information you need you're a good man and friend at the end of the day that's enough you can't think that you have to handle everyone issue just being in their life is enough at times."

"I know you right baby, and thank you for the kind words, be safe congratulations. Damn, I love you hurry your ass back."

"Love you too. Thank you and I will."

All because of that damn ring fucking exclusive one of a kind ring I should have known, my eyes don't like ordinary shit. I broke all rules and regulations made by myself because I was thinking with my heart a fucking fool in love, me of all people should know how fucking small the world really is but the ring was so different.

I noticed his ring before I even noticed him I was out on Miami Beach at a lil restaurant on the strip. I choose this spot because his file said he frequents here a lot so I figured I'd go in learn the layout along with the menu. While ordering a drink a man came up next to me talking hella loud on the phone letting everyone know his bullshit plans. I hated those types I never even looked in their direction, I don't feed wild animals. I don't like loud ass niggas so I started facing my body in the opposite direction. When my drink came he reached before I could and slide it in front of me and that's when I noticed the ring and had to look at the owner I seen the smile and then the face and just like that "Waldo" had found me.

That ring was gorgeous just like my dad's. I knew when he left the ring was leaving too I never seen nothing like it but still so similar to my dad ring. I had to get it for Tae shit this nigga wasn't gone be able to sport it no more. A two 3 ct tw square cut 24kt gold ring I was a fan of both the gold and chocolate diamonds. It would look good on my babies chocolate smooth skin. I didn't even have to touch it instead Tae could have just went to the funeral, he already family of Antonio's and could of got the ring from them his self now what I am I going to tell him how will I explain the ring he already confirmed what I already knew belonged to his friend in Miami whom he calls "A" has a ring that's custom made and looks a lot like this and I got a feeling that he knows it is his ring he gotta know I would know if I saw it and it aint even a woman ring the shit is just dope doe. I'm paranoid I can't do it I don't want him killing me and I don't want to have to kill him cause he missed his opportunity at killing me because I won't let that shit slide.

Last few weeks or whatever I been feeling like I'm walking on egg shells and to top it all off when I got back while Tae and I were on our way to eat I found Jah's DL's in his car, I was applying lip gloss when it fell on the side of the seat in search for my MAC gloss I found it.

"I got a surprise for you baby." he chimed in right when my hand touched the card.

"I'm sure it is. Who's ID is this?"

"Let me see. Oh that's my cousin she must of left it in here I dropped her off at her baby daddy crib the other day."

"Damn we should go take it to her she look young I know she's going crazy getting all kind of slack without it!"

"I'll take it to her later aint no telling where she at she be a lil bit of everywhere plus this is our time no interruptions."

"You right love, lets enjoy this time together you never know it could be one of our last!"

Now on top of me and Chrys being on top of Tae's most wanted list he done fucked around and got on mine dis nigga done had Jah ass in the car with him most definitely I found the proof wit her ratchet ass picture on it. I don't know if Tae know she's my girl or if Jah know that he's my Tae but I'm thinking she got to know she an ignorant bitch but not a stupid one. The girl can add real quick and solve puzzles like Mr. Columbus taught her himself. Maybe somebody did steal her driver license and now they lost em man fuck that this still makes Tae ass a cheater. Slippin up riding round with bitches or maybe his cousin stole it I don't know let me figure this shit out I still got Rich ass too I have to deal with and put some time in with tonight. I don't want slip up and kill his ass early from a migraine.

By the time I got to Rich my head was throbbing, my patience was short so his feisty attitude was not helping. Rich and I had been messing around for a couple months and I still hadn't slept with him yet and I would do all I could to keep it that way. Tonight I realized every little flaw that I may have noticed but never bothered me before was now screaming at me this evening. His beady eyes were just smothering me while his pale sweaty palms made my stomach turn and his five o'clock shadow tore the skin on my shoulder at least it felt like it.

"Baby what's wrong you not your usual self-tonight, you seem distant, want to talk about it?" He said pulling me in closer to him. I was about to make up some flaw ass story so I could get the hell out of dodge. My phone began to ring and from the ring tone it was Chrys that girl sometime had the best timing. Rich pulled away from me giving me the space to answer my phone.

I answered, I knew what she wanted and to be honest I was happy for the save. She had been calling me all day but I didn't answer while I was with Tae. Tomorrow was our girl day and I know she was trying to remind me since I missed it last months. With all the shit going through my head today I really almost forgot. When I got off the phone I made some shit up about girls night being tonight and I had to go because I had been neglecting my girls and that wasn't fair to me or them, I needed that bonding time in my life trying to make my way out the door. Rich was disappointed trying to get me to stay I knew he was betting on tonight being "the night" but I just wasn't feeling it after what seemed like forever he finally agreed to reschedule for the day after tomorrow and I happily obliged I knew I would have a plan all figured out by then. I left puzzling a plan together for tomorrow when I see my girls. I would need their help.

I got to Chrys house early that morning I know I shocked her that she didn't have to call me and I showed up before the other ladies. When I got there she informed me Lana wasn't coming which made me a little sad but it was cool. I had a plan and I really didn't want to use Lana but I didn't mind critique from her, but it's cool since she is would be my official lawyer one day. The less she knew the better.

We ate brunch at the Café First Watch where Jah did inform me she did lose her ID about two weeks ago she just wasn't sure where. I didn't press her because I didn't need her to be warned about what I had planned for her tomorrow. We did some shopping at International Mall then slid to Ybor where we caught a movie. And to end a busy day, we ended up at Nails True where we got our toes and nails taken care of. Chrys got her eyebrow done and Jah got them thick lashes put on while I got my fifteen minute back and shoulder beat. All in all the day was much needed and drama free which I really appreciate. Soon as we stepped back in the house I went straight for my stash it was time to woo my girls and get down to business.

"I'm glad we had our day today I'm mad Lele wasn't at the shop today and fish breath had to do my nails, but that amazon lady blew the stress out my back. she got me lose and now we ending girls day with this sleep over I missed yawl been busy as hell but this is what I needed my homies. Now that we inside one on one. I got some real personal issues in my life and who better to tell than yawl. So, yawl got my back?"

Chrys spoke first "Girl you know I do!" Jah looked at Chrys as to say damn. She looked up at me and smiled "Girl you know I'm down for whateva, aint no hoe in me."

"We know that's a lie" Chrys clapped back. She did set herself up with that one I thought while laughing lil to my surprise Jah laughed too. Which for me, was a good sign to put everything on the table for my plan for tomorrow.

"Cool so check this out. Me and Devontae...."

"Yes finally. Dirt!" Jah said sitting up straight.

"Whateva!" I said rolling my eyes continuing my plan.

\*\*\*\*\*

"Hey Mimi, what you doing up so late?" He peeked over in my cup "And drinking milk what's wrong can't go to sleep?" I pressed pause on my iPod and just looked at my dad for a couple of seconds. My dad was handsome you can see where he probably didn't get much sleep but that was it no grays I guess I didn't worry him too much average build not fat not skinny still a looker. My affliction tonight was how and if I tell him I would be leaving a while. Now with him standing in front of me at twelve thirty midnight gave me my answer cause pops usually be sleep by now.

"I was thinking of taking a lil vacation tomorrow I need some me time. I just want to go away see what's out there for me. I'm twenty-one it's time to explore."

"OK so where you going and how long?"

"I don't know yet but I'm almost sure I'm leavin tomorrow."

"Well let me know so I can rent out your room" He said with a giggle "It's hard out here"

"You are a mess. I don't know where I get it from

you or mom but we always about a dollar."

"Shit, you gotta be now a days the price to something always going up by time you wake up. Are you OK Mimi? Do you want to or do you have to?"

"I need to."

"Well if you need help protection guidance I know a lot of people."

"I think I can handle myself I have had an awesome instructor a no bullshit having always living in reality type person."

"Thank you Mimi but I think someone or something else changed you I'm just glad it wasn't for the worst. You will always have a key to my house and a bed in my home. OK?"

"OK. Thank you. I love you dad."

"Love you too Mimi. Don't stay up too late"

"I won't. I gotta say bye to some people tomorrow, good night." I turned my music up and zoned back out cleaning my dishes and making my way up the stairs off to the roof to smoke my doobie. *"I'm trying to decide which way to go I think I made a wrong turn back there somewhere I said you never know which way the cards will lay....."* Life is defiantly a ride we stay just riding at least I do. Damn I love Erykah Badu and the truth in her words.

Netta B.

# Chapter Twenty one

May 2013

Today was the day I been setting shit up in my mind the last two days I was ready to get all this unnecessary unprofitable shit in my life done and over with, put my focus back on me. Tae, Rich, and Jah we were all about to reach an understanding today.

When I pulled back up to Rich's Mansion he was already there and all I'd done was run to the corner store for a money card. There he was standing outside at the bottom of the stairs holding a single red rose. Rich looked kinda good standing up there I don't know if the raw veggie fruit smoothies and a couple homemade baked and grilled meals that had him shining or if it was that Armani suit with matching shoes those Gucci cuff links or the 18kt presidential on his arm I parked my Panomera Porsche hopped out in my Fendi dress, Louboutin heels, Hermes clutch, and a big smile and strutted to this fool. He handed me the rose then picked up a box wrapped in the funny papers and bow made out the comics too, it was so neat and so creative I had to see what was inside and I loved it was a Sapphire Movado all black, told him a couple days ago while flipping through GQ magazine I wanted that watch and not the women's cut I want this one were my words and bent the corners so there would be no mix up.

"Thank you fat daddy."

"You are more than welcome, now come on in." He

opened the door and had two chilled wine glasses sitting by the door I guess he'd been inside too.

"Hey Juno baby you look beautiful."

"Thanks baby you're not looking bad yourself Mr. GQ"

"Well beauty shall we. He sat at the dinner table while I prepared the plates.

"So Juno how's the job you ready to quit yet?"

"More than you ever know. Now it's cutting into my sleep how can I be Sleeping Pretty if I never get any sleep."

"You my dear will always be pretty as long as you have me you will never have a worry care or a stressful day in your life."

"You really know what to say and how to treat a princess you are my knight and shining armor."

"And you my princess."

"This night is to us a grand beginning so let's enjoy it!"

"Yea lets and something is smelling so good."

"Well I wonder what it is? Let's take a look and see!" I said smiling I was hungry as hell at the moment anyway. "We have your favorite lasagna garlic bread corn on the cob, if you not up for the pasta taste and want to stick to your diet I baked some chicken, there's rice and chicken base gravy with cornbread. And for dessert your favorite strawberry cake from Publix. I'm going to have some cheesy greasy bad lasagna, what kind of plate you want?"

"Um I think I'll have the same, now go so we can dig in before it gets too cold."

"I know rite!" I said hurrying to the kitchen. I knew his greedy ass would say lasagna I had two plates already prepared and sitting in the warm oven. Right after I scrubbed down the kitchen again paying attention to whatever I just touched I grabbed our plates and headed back in the dining room. I poured us a fresh glass of wine mine red he liked white and sat down ready to eat before our fun filled night began. Rich grabbed my hand for grace but before he started I interrupted him.

"Uh Rich I know you always say grace but let me this time honey." He looked a little surprised and happy, I don't know what that was about. "Heavenly father I come to you in prayer to thank you for this wonderful meal that has been prepared help it to nourish our bodies and souls. Thank you for the bonding. Guild us and please continue to forgive us because we are truly fools that do not understand our greatness. Amen."

"So you do pray huh."

"God is good."

"All the time! Can you believe It's only been a couple months maybe bout a half of year, and I feel so close to you. I get you I understand you I want to love and take care of you."

"I know right it's been great and fun a learning experience good and bad."

"What do you mean by that good and bad?"

"I say good because you've helped me grow showed me so many things and places taught me the game don't take nothing personal and keep everyone close to you. Stay business minded even about the little things keep an open eye and ear to people you meet because you never know when a business opportunity may present itself. Money waits for no man not even a woman. I say bad because I've never dated a white man and the stares the comments about me being too fine for a white man people telling me you're not serious about me because I'm so young not established yet. I became entangled in you and forgot about my friends and family, people who really know me. So I've learned some things is all I'm saying let's get stuffed."

"Well eat woman I haven't stopped eating yet this is good Juno. I feel relaxed ready for glass two of wine."

"I'll go pour it for you"

During dinner I just thought. My mind was racing a mile a minute was I moving too fast should I have waited. What was I going to do I already put some things in place and from the way Rich sounded at the moment things were already in motion. What do I want? What is my next step, how can I make this work? How do I tell Tae, will he be OK with it? Will his feelings completely change for me? Can he grasp the emotional and mental release of payback? Sure he will, I know he done did some dirt must of bust at least one burner. He's a business man he knows a job is a hustle and a hustle is a job. Money never stops and determination never fails. We all got something we after, and a lot of shit good and bad came with a chase.

I would have to get very personal and tell him everything, starting back in Detroit. But he'd really have to know and understand about Javon and our personal relationship. What he did and how much he meant to me, he would have to understand my deepest thoughts. I know the way his friend was killed is what's really putting a toll on him. I'd tell it all starting back in Detroit beginning with Corey ending with Mr. Jay and lastly the loss of my best friend Javon. I'd tell him I caught up with Corey he was my first taste of revenge and work it into how I got Javon killer and this one was serious and very personal to me. How I never tortured anyone but I had to with this one he caused me a lot of pain so I paid him back in full I never took anything from a scene or left any signatures behind that wasn't my style I left a clean scene and took no ties to it. But for him I needed to remember this I wanted a piece of him a souvenir if you will so I took his ring.

Maybe he would try and kill me maybe it would take a minute to soak in. Maybe he would understand want to nurture and protect me. Shit all I know I going up north, and after I deal with Rich ass I'm a have to deal with Tae aint no way around it. Can't and won't live a lie. All together at the end of the day I was tired I came here early this morning and clean every inch of this house never really had too many things here so it was a light pack. I just wanted to get this night over with. And Rich ass over here don't make me feel no better give no energy I'm ready to put him out his misery.

"That was good now it's time for desert.'

"Daddy please go get it." I said preparing him another wine glass.

"Lasagna strawberry cake and wine I don't know if my body can handle this it might be going into shock. You know what comes after a good meal and drinks right."

"Yea I know, but I don't know if you are ready. I said with the sexist laugh I could muster. Plus you are not getting any of this good ass loving just yet we still have to catch that play. You could take a few more bites that may satisfy your sweet tooth or at least finish your wine you gotta be on my level to keep up with me tonight we gone party...lets go to the living room watch the dumb dumb box and eat this before we leave"

"You're the boss."

"You damn right!" When Rich stood up he swayed a little but caught his balance just shaking off that little stumble.

"Damn baby what year is that wine from because the way I feel it must have been a grand ass year." He made his way to the couch plopping down in the middle lifting one leg then motioned for me to come sit by him by lifting his arm up. I scooted up under him waiting for him to pass out or something he didn't he just continued to drink which worked in my favor when he was done he reached to put the glass on the coffee table but just dropped his arm to his side then looked over my way. "Damn baby I don't feel too good. If I didn't know better I'd think you put something in my food or drink."

"Well thank goodness you know me better than that big daddy."

"Really though somethings not right Juno. Oh lord your food done made me sick Juno baby."

"Stop playing you probably just gotta shit. It's OK. Just relax and let it work itself out." I said with a giggle. "Here sit your other foot up and relax."

"That's the thing I am relaxed so relaxed I feel heavy."

*You damn rite and glad it wasn't sooner or I would've had to drag you to this couch I thought* "Stop playing you're not trying to get out of plans tonight are you?"

"Look I can barely left my hand" He said barely able to grip his glass already in hand. "Go into my office and look up Dr. Hart call him now Dr. Cecil hart. GO. Hurry up!" His speech was beginning to sound like a drunken language.

"OK. Cecil Hart" I repeated. I darted off like I was really bout to help this fool I stopped at the bathroom instead. I fixed a few strands of hair, sponged my face, reapplied my gloss then took a little off washed my hands then posed in the mirror wanted to take a pic for IG but that would of been evidence of being here. Man I looked good those smoothies and planks had my lil low ass baby gut gone I was just tighter. I searched and found some gloves from under the bathroom sink slipping them on posing in the mirror like I was a doctor "Damn girl you are pretty" I said to myself before I called Chrys to tell her everything was still in order to go head and call Jah and Tae.

*Action.* "Oh my god I called and called left several messages hopefully he's the type of doctor to call right back." He could barely shake his head so I knew he couldn't talk it was time for me to explain everything so I could talk and not be interrupted with questions. I sat on the coffee table in front of him propped one leg on the side of him and began explaining.

"Now Rich...I like you. You are all right with me you take care of yours I've experienced it first-hand. So I hate to have to do wrong by you. I slipped something into your drink three times tonight so you should be pretty doped up. I have two messages to you tonight. One: it's not good to keep a secret and if you do keep a secret and if no one knows that's secret IT will or can come back and bit you. I was a fun secret though wasn't I? And two you never tell people eating at another table your recipe. You told me a complete stranger who you know absolutely nothing about besides what I told you, everything. I could take your whole life away from you. The shit pillow talk brings up, aren't you glad you signed everything you own or did own over to your daughter. From what I know about you, or your "likes" there is no doubt in my mind she ultimately deserves it." while talking my shit his phone vibrated that caught me off guard this whole time I've known him I never heard his phone make a peep.

"Oh and that might be her let me see." I said reaching for his phone from the clip of his waist. "What the fuck! Come talk to over 100 hot young girls....man you are truly something else what type of shit you on where you get text bout hot young girls. You really are sick! At least I had you dress nice and pretty for whomever found you. We could have worked it out if you weren't so disgusting you so thirsty for young ass and think you're so untouchable I would of let you live just went and did it his way but you may get some weak minded girl and take that stuff that you do overboard and hurt somebody. I've smell the scent of others on you and it's not full blown woman. So you gotta go. Some of the names you called me and things you made me do. Unforgivable just like what I'm about to do to you still I ask the lord to forgive me and you for we are truly fools." *Father forgive me.* A clean shot to the head that's all it took. I didn't really want to mess up his suit. It was only a matter of time before somebody got a hold on em. I heard Jah loud Camaro pulling up and I went to go meet her at the door.

"Girl you be fucking wit some real G's look at this house this shit dope dis where you was at when you said you was in New Port Richey huh?" She said walking thru the front door. "Yea you aint gotta answer I know. I'm sorry he crossed paths with you doe!"

"I know right! I'm glad I got loyal friends and shit who don't talk or fuck around behind my back." I paused mainly to watch her body movements and listen if she wanted to say anything. She didn't just continue to go in the house and look around. "I can trust yawl that's what's up."

"Oh damn Mimi I know this dude! Damn he a nasty Cracka, I'd kill his ass too!"

"Damn you know everybody! You probably would a ratted me out to get dough too, I'm glad you aint know he was my mark. So what you tell Tae?" She turned and looked at me like bitch what?

"What? Girl I don't know him."

"What you talking about hoe I found your ID in his car."

Looking confused she turned to face me. "I know I been trippin and shit lately real slick with the tongue, but I aint no backstabber. I lost my ID shid I told you that I think I lost it at Hush. I know you a killa you aint gotta test me. I haven't told anybody anything about you...I don't know who Tae is killa. I know dead man but not your man."

Damn I felt kind of bad. She was looking scared worried hurt unsure but not guilty on top of that looking me dead in the eyes. "I'm sorry but I told you if I felt betrayal and an ID is a big ass clue if you ask me, but I'm sorry. I just wanted to make sure. Bump it." I gave her a little hug to ease her a bit. Then told her to go clean that table and kitchen those dishes we just ate from the glasses dining room table and chairs and the wine bottle gave her some dish gloves and one last order of don't touch the body or anything around it. Would of gave her my hair net but that was weave on her head good luck to the CSI unit finding that horse.

On my way back to the bathroom I thought Tae would be here soon damn he was so fucking sexy I loved that nigga I don't think I could kill him if it came down to it, I hope we would have an understanding of it all in the end. I began cleaning the knobs and any hair that may have shed when it looked good enough I headed to the guest room to get the last bag I packed it was for Jah $500,000 just found it in his office and a safe he had in the house. It was hers Jah could have it all if she passed this last little test. I hated her tricking and doing drops. I loved my homie but I just couldn't stand her ass lately.

"Mina, Mina! Girl where you at!?" That was Tae right on time. Speed walking into the foyer, I seen Jah creeping peeking over the corner at Tae who was looking round all frantic when he seen me he began walking my way when he turned to see what I was looking at. He spotted Jah they looked at each other but that was that no emotion no recognition no nothing. Damn aint no way they know each other, but how the fuck did her shit get in his whip? I figure that out later.

"What the fuck happened here!?" Tae started us off. "This nigga over on the couch leaking blood, she in there washing dishes and shit and what you doing back there taking a evening nap or some shit?"

"It's all good we just cleaning up. Had to take him out a little earlier than we planned I was getting tired of him." Tae eyes looked like they were going to explode out of his eye socket.

"Mina we had a plan." His voice was calm but he looked like he could of slapped the shit out of me.

"If you mad about the money don't worry about it, I'm Rich beyond your hood dreams."

"Lucky bitch." We both looked at Jah. She was posted. Just leaning all on the wall like we were acting in her favorite movie.

"Who is she?"

"Khadijah one of the homies of the fabulous four. Jah this Tae." I said hoping to make the tension a little lighter in the air.

"Can you give us a min Khadijah?" Tae chimed in.

"Whatever nigga this aint yo house, yawl two made for each other. A Bossy negro and a Bitch guess that make yall the Boss Bitch!" She said with much attitude while walking off. Guess that didn't work Tae was now slightly more irritated then before and I didn't think that was possible.

"Look Tae if it's about the product I know where he got it stored. I found out everything you wanted to know I'm not just your baby girl I'm your boss ass woman shit you should know I got my man back. He smiled a little but it quickly went away. He just kind of blankly stared at me. His stare was cold I felt very uncomfortable I looked off to verify what I thought I'd just seen in the corner of my eye and it was correct Jah had made her way back into the dining room and was back in her spot chillin and didn't seem to care that I spotted her. I really didn't give a fuck either. I focused back on Tae "Look I gotta tell you something I made a decision today that I should just leave so I figure I'd go up to Detroit for a little while just till shit cool off round here. You are more than welcome I mean I would die if you didn't come, you can expand businesses of yours we..."

"Hell naw I don't want to go wit...I know people in high places I'll be OK...my dawg my homie tho?" That made me stand a little straighter, he was looking like he was stating facts but it sounded like a question a why. "In Miami I had no luck. My folks couldn't find out which pawn shop you got the ring from if they did sell it they didn't write it down or snap a picture."

"I'm sure they'll find the sho..."

"And a broad killed him. Some chick he that he just met, he only knew her a couple days. My cousin said he bragging bout some chick he just met how fine she was. What can make you befriend someone just to kill em?" Again this sounded like a question that was directed to me. "I mean the way she took my homie out it was like it personal or some shit.

"Well I'm sure they will find her it's cameras on damn near every corner nowadays."

"They did catch her." My eyes were bullets shooting up to meet his. "I mean not physically but on a video tape."

"See that's good. That's a good start only a matter of time now."

"Yea, you right. She had red hair and big bifocal ass glasses, but that walk she just floated didn't miss a beat it was like I knew that walk it was seductive but business. It was on my mind all day until I seen you, you took all that hurt up out of me brought me joy and I remembered I got something I never get caught up by a broad cause I got the best at home. When I came home from Miami you greeted me with hugs and kiss massaging my back and shoulders cooked the best dinner you made ever. Then you said let's roll play you sat me in a chair you blind folded me and when you came back to take the blindfold off there she was Ms. Red Pepper the red lipstick, red thigh highs, red heels, red nails, and red hair so sexy ironic the color you choose but I figured oh well red is the color of love it was a coincidence. You were here to ease me I was ready to see red all night. So I went with the flow but I couldn't get that image out my head so I had you go turn on my shit I said you know I like to fuck to the beat you giggled and walked off that walk away is what gave it all away. I knew it was you in the tape. I mean why not? You had the ring the red hair you were gone that week. I just didn't want to believe it."

"That's what I wanted to talk about."

"What!? Talk to me about what? You just gone sit me down tell me you killed my friend then we gone go catch late dinner or movie."

"I was gone tell you a story, from beg..."

"A story bitch I don't want to hear no fucking story." *Yea he done lost his mind nigga called me a bitch.*

"No. Tae let me finish I was gone tell you about me it's a lot of things you don't know I just wanted to explain tell you where A.P. fit into the picture."

"A.P.? A.P.?! Don't call my dawg by his nickname like yawl go way back. Bitch you fucking wit me?" *There go that Bitch word again.* "Yea you fucking with me you plan on killing me too huh. Is this a fucking game you playing bitch?"

"No Tae I love you, I care for you. You came for me not the other way around."

"I saw the way you was looking at that picture at my peeps house you was froze you just stared I knew something was up then but I thought you knew who did it, maybe fucked one of the homies something, not the sick bitch who slit his dick off."

"I..."

"I don't care bout shit you got to say, I don't trus..." Before he could even finish his sentence to lie on me and say I'm not to be trusted. Jah blew a hole in the back of that nigga head.

"Girl he was finna shoot yo ass. You aint catch that nigga damn near had the gun on yo eye now. Good thing I got this burner before I came out here I know you said I didn't need one but I guess you never huh. "

"I know...thank you. I was slipping." I knew what just happened but I was frozen though. Love had me trippin Jah ass just saved me.

"Guess he forgot my ass was behind him." Jah said going back to the kitchen. "You bet not touch that nigga killa. I'm sorry it went down like that I'm almost done we gotta hurry up and get the fuck up out of here."

Damn. Loyalty. My dawg put a bullet in this nigga head and aint never bust a pistol before in her life, we go to the gun range all the time but her ass sits in the back watching holding the ear muffs and shit I didn't know she had it in her but I appreciate her. Shit like that is why she in my life in the first place and why she a half a million dollars richer. She always had my back from day one.

PRETTY: Her Introduction

# Chapter Twenty two

May 2013

Patricia Dodson
Age: 33
Race: White
Height: 5'7
Weight: 142

Address: 1845 Nome St.
Detroit, Mich. 36781

Employment: Ballet dancer, singer,
entertainer
Hobbies: golf, swimming, skating, and arts
Interest: performance arts, history,
entertainment, and fashion

Patricia Dodson is a ballet dancer lives alone
has two kids who reside with their father. All
family is Detroit bred natives as well as her.
She has molest young girls and kills them she
never been convicted of crime subject
believes her daughter was one of the targets
victims because of some words that were

**exchanged at ballet class. She is said to have
and sex addiction and OCD, but her rage and
anger towards little girls are strictly jealousy
acts afraid of being replaced. She hangs out
at the dinner red lips every other day.**

### Expiration date 2 week from now THE SOONER
### THE BETTER
### Completion call 8185555187 ext. 187

I never really came up North often for work it was
very seldom. Not that there less child abuse cases up here
it's just folk up here tend to handle their own business I
guess, that's the only conclusion I can come up with. Shit
I'm from the North and I'm a killa could be something in
the water. Most of my work was down South or West
Coast a lot of Rich fancy folk them mob boys type shit.
People who said fuck the police, fuck the courts money
will get me my justice and keep my freedom. It felt good
being back in my city and my next hit was out here in the
area, pretty close to where I use to live, isn't that ironic.
Could be a sign or could just be. I was feeling
spontaneous. I wanted to try something different
probably because I felt different happy, sad, and
everything between and around it.

Two men very different but quite the same in my
heart were taken away from me maybe I should just wait
till I'm done with all my dirty work then focus on a man.
It hurt to have to leave Tae there bleeding to death right
in Rich house I figured he would come with me. I figured
he would listen and understand but he didn't he was

angry I was the new and they were the old they had seniority which meant just a little bit more than I did. That is how my mom should of acted with me and Corey I should of automatically had her trust over him but that was neither here or there and very over with. This morning a single black rose was sent to my phone from an anonymous sender. I never verified if Tae was dead, didn't want to look at him let alone touch him to check his pulse. Only time will tell.

After my hit in a couple of days I'm planning on surprising my mom at the shop like what up doe my baby! I know she would love that shit. I'm a stick around make some tax money so I don't have the IRS after me. I'm on my way to Detroit Opera House going all out tonight. Got a seat front row and a backstage pass, single tonight, a Mimi night. Who knows maybe I'll meet up with a Jah, Chrys, and Lana the Detroit version. The thought of that was funny and scary and I'm sure a hell of a lot of action, shit we cut throat up here every man for self and theirs. T baby could not have said it any better "It's so cold in the D". It feels good to back in my city and I'm already helping with cleaning of the streets. Thanks to Rich's paper work in his little Gardall Fb safe I found out about all type of people from papers he had, my very own little history lesson. Contestant number three Mr. J was out here in my old hometown and I heard he was doing his thing in the game a number one player. It was time for him to meet the coach, Mr. J I'm on ya ass.

Turn down for what!?